YES, YES, CHERRIES

stories by

MARY OTIS

Tin House Books

Published by Tin House Books, Portland, Oregon,
and New York, New York

Distributed to the trade by Publishers Group West,
1700 Fourth St., Berkeley, CA 94710, www.pgw.com

Library of Congress Cataloging-in-Publication Data

Otis, Mary, 1961–
Yes, yes, cherries : stories/Mary Otis.—1st U.S. ed.
p. cm.
ISBN 978-0-9776989-0-5
I. Title.
PS3615.T57Y47 2007
813'.6—dc22
2006100131

DESIGNED BY PAULINE NEUWIRTH, NEUWIRTH & ASSOCIATES, INC.

First U.S. edition 2007

ISBN 10: 0–9776989–0–4

www.tinhouse.com

Thanks to the editors of the following publications, where some of the
stories in this collection first appeared, sometimes in earlier versions:
"Pilgrim Girl" and "Unstruck" in *Tin House*;
"Five-Minute Hearts" in *Best New American Voices 2004;*
"Welcome to Yosemite" in *Cincinnati Review;*
"Stones" in *Berkeley Literary Journal*.

Printed in Canada

FOR JIM KRUSOE,
A WONDERFUL TEACHER

CONTENTS

YES, YES, CHERRIES

PILGRIM GIRL

FOR ANOTHER SECOND Allison is safe. She's outside the Wingerts' house, and the front door is still shut. But Janie Wingert is coming down the hallway, her tasteful heels clicking on the terra-cotta tiles, and Allison has dressed up as a traveling saleswoman, though she doesn't know why. She has no products. Why didn't this occur to her before now? It seemed like a great idea when she was in her bedroom, not raking her shag rug, the thing she was supposed to do when she got home from band practice. It seemed like a great idea to root the frosted-blond wig out of her mother's stocking drawer, where her mother hid it after the Lions Club Mardi Gras party. It seemed like a great idea to jam it on her head and walk across the street.

Janie Wingert opens the door, holding her orange cat, Mr. Teddy. Janie is in sales, real sales, important sales that include clients, accounts, quotas, and jumping on planes, and this occurs to Allison, the unreal salesperson, too late. Janie looks at Allison in her band blazer and the black funeral skirt that she filched from her mother's "occasional wear" drawer.

What was Allison thinking? Perhaps she was trying to "get out of herself," something her mother made her write on a piece of paper last Sunday—"I, Allison, will try to get out of myself"—and sign and affix to the refrigerator.

"Hi, Janie," Allison says. "I'm a saleswoman." And she can see the look in Janie's eyes, the kind she would, for example, give a Hare Krishna, the sort of individual that Allison recently heard Janie describe to her mother as a "tangled soul." Though Allison suspects Janie would just as soon kick a Hare Krishna as look at one.

Janie is deft at appearing out of herself. She pries Mr. Teddy from her shoulder, Mr. Teddy of the six toes on each foot and the continually shell-shocked look, and holds him in her arms, as if he were a homecoming queen bouquet.

"What are you selling, Allison?" Janie says as she stares at Allison's white vinyl and yellow-flowered overnight bag, which Allison grabbed at the last minute as a sales prop.

"What you need to buy, Janie." Allison is completely aware of her crummy sales technique. Mr. Teddy, who is generally inactive, suddenly bats one paw in her direction.

Janie squints at Allison and begins to back away from the door. Then she stops and says, "Rick, honey, come here. Allison from across the street is trying to be funny or something."

And then it hits Allison. Rick. Rick. Janie's husband who has a blond beard and works at an insurance company, but seems very outdoorsy nonetheless, the type that she could easily see as a carpenter, for one day Allison hopes to move to California and marry a carpenter. It's Rick. The reason she is pretending to be a traveling saleswoman. Again, this occurs to her too late.

"Hey, Allison, what's shakin'?" Rick always knows just what to say. Once, when Allison was riding her bike home from school, Rick asked her if she was all right and she said she was, and Rick said she seemed totally depressed. That was one of the happiest days of her life, so far.

"What's the good word?" Rick takes a bite from a roll in his hand. It seems more exotic than the rolls at Allison's house. It has seeds. She looks at the bread between his index finger and thumb, how he's squeezing it just a little bit, ever so gently in between each bite.

Suddenly her head is itchy. Sweat runs down the back of her neck.

"What's in that suitcase of yours?" Rick asks. And Allison remembers that she hid her sketch in there, the one she's been working on for two months, entitled "A Woman's Mind." Allison is a terrible artist, but she has taken great nightly comfort in working on this picture of a woman's brain that extends upward like a multilayered parking lot, on each level squeezing in all kinds of sub-versive thoughts and romantic hopes, each of them encoded in strange symbols that would mean nothing to anyone but her. Still, she hid it. Rick must not see this.

"Products," she whispers.

"Allison," Rick says. "Allison, you're a real laugh riot."

AT HOME, ALLISON'S mother and Aunt Tuley are waiting in the kitchen for her. Tonight is the last night of the Fam-ily Fun Expo at the mall, and her mother really, really wants the three of them to go to a costume photo booth called "Old-Fashioned Days" and get their picture taken as pilgrim ladies because they live only two towns away from Ply-mouth, Massachusetts, because this photo could have Christ-mas card potential.

"Where have you been, Allison?" asks her mother.

"Trying out for the seventh-grade play," Allison says, using the fabulous excuse she cooked up while crossing the street from Janie and Rick's driveway to her own, and already she sees that her mother is fixated on the fact that she's wear-ing her wig and funeral skirt. But for a moment Allison has special powers. She has been referred to as a laugh riot by a twenty-four-year-old man.

"Well, that's a step in the right direction," says Aunt Tuley. Aunt Tuley is her mother's younger sister. "Much younger," Tuley will always add. Tuley is only eight years older than Allison. She was voted Most Pert in her high school yearbook. "What play?" she says.

"A new play."

"About?" says Allison's mother.

"About salespeople," Allison says. There's a horrible feeling inside the wig, as if there are warm scrambled eggs on top of her head. She'd mushed down her long brown hair with Vaseline, such was her eagerness to get that blond shag wig on her skull.

"I could see you onstage," says Aunt Tuley, lying.

That's not a thing that would come to anyone's mind, Allison thinks. She's too still, for one thing. Actresses move around a lot. She has dead arms.

"Though you are a little static." Aunt Tuley is an English major at Salem State College, and she constantly throws around her "Power People" vocabulary words.

Allison bursts into tears. Aunt Tuley and her mother are both so used to this that neither one reacts, and her mother, not even looking at her, pours her a bowl of Apple Jacks to eat in the car on the way to the mall. Allison watches Tuley and her mother walk out the door, and she stands there, crying in her hot wig with her dead arms. And it's completely out of the question that her mother's going to wait in the car while she changes out of her traveling saleswoman getup. Allison yanks the wig off her head and savagely whips it across the kitchen table. Then she picks up the bowl of Apple Jacks and dumps it in the trash, a pathetically tiny "fuck you," and every bit of her newfound, Rick-induced composure has vanished, as if she never had it at all.

⸺⁂⸺

NO ONE IS at the "Old-Fashioned Days" booth except Dee Deluca, who works there every year for extra cash. Dee, a professional drill team coach, can often be seen stomping around downtown with a canvas sack of batons over her shoulder. Might as well be a sack of guns.

Dee tells Allison's mother there's only one female pilgrim costume left. There used to be more, being that they were so popular, but people ripped them off.

Aunt Tuley has the brilliant idea that Allison will be the one and only pilgrim girl, and before Allison knows it, she's in a dowdy black dress that smells like K2r spot remover, and Dee presses something that looks like a doily on her head and slowly rotates it as if she's screwing in a lightbulb. Allison remembers that she's heard rumors about Dee, how she'll tie a girl's wrists to her baton with fishing wire if she drops it in practice. And when she hands Allison a fake stone mortar and pestle with its grubby Pier One sticker half-melted off, Allison doesn't want to touch this item that in part reminds her of a tiny stone penis, but she takes it anyway, and when Dee commands her to hold it directly in front of her belly button, she keeps it there. Allison doesn't mention to Dee that the pilgrim costume is basically bogus, that pilgrims actually wore colors. She read that in one of her favorite magazines, *The Young Historian*.

Dee fiddles with the camera, and asks, "How tall are you, miss?"

"Five-eight," answers Allison.

"Tall. That's tall for a pilgrim girl," says Dee, as if she's doing them a big favor. Allison closes her eyes, and all around her, she hears the swish of voices.

"Open your eyes," says Aunt Tuley. "Don't be churlish."

How powerful of you to say that, Tuley, and through her closed eyelids Allison sends electric hate beams.

"Open them, Allison, don't be childish," and Allison gets some small satisfaction that her mother has misrepeated Tuley. And she's about to open her eyelids. But just before she does, she has a moment such as she's never had before, and as it happens, the outside of herself completely drops away, and she is suddenly and completely in her own underneath, a quiet place where her hidden softness and wonder are gathered and kept in waiting for someday, somewhere, another person on earth to know.

And then, again, she is Pilgrim Girl. One shot is taken with mortar and pestle and one without. Tuley goes to smoke a cigarette outside the Ross Dress for Less loading dock, and Dee comes in for the big kill now that she has Allison's mother alone. Dee is pushing this horrible faux-wood frame on her mother that costs three times what the pictures themselves did, and Allison can see that Dee is wearing her down. And she feels sad for her mother, because she knows she'll buy it.

On the way home, Allison sits in the backseat and looks at the picture, which Tuley said looks austere. "Austere in a good way." Each time they pass a streetlight Allison frantically tilts her photograph and studies it, and each time she hopes to, but does not, see loveliness.

⸺ ⸙ ⸻

ALLISON HAS BEEN working on a campaign to get people to call her Ali, pronounced like the boxer. The extent of her efforts amounts to writing *Ali, Ali,* in Magic Marker on the inside heel of both her sneakers, which she has just done while listening to Janie Wingert call Mr. Teddy into the house before she leaves for work.

Ali looks good. *Ali* has punch. *Allison*—a downward leaning, collapsed bridge of a name—has nothing to do with her. She saw the school bus come and go, but her shoes haven't dried, and Allison looks out her bedroom window and sees Janie standing in her driveway.

"Come here, Mr. Teddy . . ." calls Janie. "Mr. Teddy? Mr. Teddy WONderful . . ."

Rick walks out the front door and Allison thinks she can see that he's had just about enough. She predicts the demise of Rick and Janie's marriage. Too much cat sweet talk. Husbands and wives need to save their kindest words for each other, even when tired or hungry. She read this in the September *Family Circle.*

Rick opens his car door and puts a bag lunch and a large black organizer on the front seat. Rick is a supervisor. Supervising is sexy. And Allison is sure that with just a few small changes Rick could make that leap to being a carpenter. Carpenters hammer alone, supervisors walk down halls alone. Because it doesn't pay to fraternize in that sort of position. This much she knows from her mother, who, though not a supervisor, works as an office manager in a dentist's office. She is "pleasant" to the patients, but she doesn't fraternize with them.

"Mr. Teddy?" and Allison sees Janie standing there in her gray dress that starts narrow at the top, but circles out at the bottom, and she thinks how very much she looks like a little lighthouse, what with her slender shoulders and her moronic head swinging back and forth like a beacon over the same part of the yard that she just looked at five times.

Then Allison sees Mr. Teddy Wonderful sitting to the side of the house, just out of Janie's view, unmoving, staring at air. And she could knock-knock-knock on the window and help old Janie out. She could.

Janie starts to get in her car, but before she does, she cleverly pulls a sweep of her dress fabric to the side with her thumb and index finger. So dainty, Allison thinks, so unlike the way she sits down first, then hurriedly and sneakily tries to snatch fabric from under her butt. No wonder people buy things from Janie. Allison feels crying coming on. She stops and inhales Magic Marker for distraction and looks to the *Ali* heel markings for reinforcement.

Then she puts her feet in her shoes and thinks of the secret of her new and improved name tucked between her sock and tennis shoe. She does not foresee that by the end of the day, her socks will be stained blue, her *Ali*s mangled and blurred, nothing left but a broken-down *i* in her right shoe, even its dot rolled away.

Allison runs down the stairs and out her front door, because there may be a moment after Janie backs out when Rick goes back into the house for something. It has happened before.

Allison has pictured him striding back into his kitchen, which, still smelling of waffles and coffee, has settled into the hush of a day's wait. And that's when she imagines herself suddenly appearing in the lovely, quiet kitchen with him, as if she's always lived there, and right away he pulls her into the living room, and lies down on the couch with her and holds her. And this is the thing she thinks of every single day in the time between watching Janie's Jetta pull out of the driveway and flying out the door of her own house, finding most often the gaping emptiness of the Wingerts' driveway and Rick's blue Jeep, already at the corner stop sign, stopping not for her.

But today she is lucky. Rick's coffee cup sits on the hood of the engine, and he's searching for something in the front seat. He pulls his head out just as she comes to the end of her driveway.

"Hi, Allison, how's business?" Rick smiles at her, and she gets a little scared because he's wearing a dress shirt, and this throws her off. She scrambles to think of some laugh-riot thing to say about products. All she can think of is a TV commercial about alarm clocks.

"Fine," she says.

"Do you want a lift?" He says this to her as if he gives her lifts all the time. A lift: slick and elegant, unlike what her mother gives her: a ride, with the *r* wrenched out of her mouth in a specific, exhausted way.

"Do you want me to drive across the street to get you?" And Allison realizes she hasn't answered him, and she is completely aware that this is a joke, but sadly, her mouth has broken.

"Or you can walk. If you need the time alone." No one—no one—has ever suggested that she needs this. Rick turns away, and Allison wants to sob at the sight of his back.

Then suddenly she is across the street and in the Jeep. She'll be unable to recall how she got there when she replays this moment on her continuous brain feed as soon as fifteen minutes from now.

The car rolls out of the driveway, and Allison is in love with this moment, with the way the tires bounce over a bit of uneven pavement, with the way Rick puts his hand on the back of her seat as he turns his head to look at oncoming traffic, with the way the Jeep stalls, and how when Rick shifts, the car shoots forward a little, and Rick laughs. Her life has burst open, and she feels a gush of love for the door handle of the Jeep, which she is clutching.

"Would you like a sip of coffee?" Rick asks Allison.

Her arms feel like swollen water balloons. "Only if it's leaded." Her mother's line.

"Leaded with a little milk and two sugars." Rick hands her his Allstate Insurance mug. The mug isn't hot, and she sets it down on her crotch. She doesn't know why. She instantly feels between her legs a small circle of heat begin to spin, and Allison wills it to stop, but the circle only flies tighter in upon itself. She stops breathing.

"I'm sorry," says Rick. "Do you not drink coffee?"

"No, I do. I do." She puts her palm over the top of the mug. Another bad choice. She might as well have put her hand down her pants. Allison is sure he knows everything. She still doesn't think she's breathing.

The two drive in complete silence for nine minutes. Rick stops at the stoplight in front of Cappy's Clam Shack.

"They're closing next week for the season," says Rick, looking out the window. Cappy's is halfway to school, and Allison is aware that already it's almost over, this perfect lift, this holding of a lettered mug, this almost-drinking of coffee.

She lifts the mug to her navel and holds it there, as she did her Pilgrim Girl pestle, and she remembers Dee Deluca telling her to hold it "naturally, as if it was something you touched all the time." She keeps the mug very straight. Still, she does not drink the coffee.

"I love their fried clams, and I surely miss them in the winter," says Rick. To *surely* miss something indicates to Allison great sensitivity. *Now* is the time to drink his coffee to signal her understanding. But she can't. And she doesn't know why. And the space between her legs seems as if it's opened into her lap, which now feels like a tumble of warm socks.

"What do you think, Allison, do their fried clams rate in your book?"

"I've never had them." Her mother calls Cappy's "Crappy's." She isn't allowed to eat there.

Rick pulls into the school yard. Allison desperately tries to think of some impressive food she once ate.

Rick turns his head to look at her, and she sees up close that the middle of one eyebrow is missing. She looks at the little skin road, which zags at a diagonal toward his nose. Belatedly she gets a hit of Dial soap off his beard. She tries to enjoy it, since she fears she'll never get this close again.

"Did Mr. Teddy cut your eyebrow?" she asks, hoping.

"No, I fell on a dock when I was ten. But Mr. Wonderful *did* do this," and he holds up his right hand and shows her a scratch on his knuckle. "Though Janie doesn't care. That cat's her baby."

The Jeep idles in front of the entrance to Allison's school, and Rick looks at her, waiting, waiting for something. And maybe it's his mug of coffee. But unfortunately, she just rolled down the window and dumped it out, and some of it's dripping down the side of his Jeep, and she can't believe she did that, because when she was little, her mother and Tuley used to drive to New York City in the middle of the night, and they wouldn't stop at a public restroom and they made her pee in a juice can and dump it, and she *never* hit the car.

She weighs the benefits of telling Rick this story.

"Well, I guess that's that," he says as Allison hands him his empty mug.

"I'm sorry," she says and offers to run into the school snack bar to get him an orange juice or chocolate milk.

"Don't sweat it," and Rick pats her thigh, and her lap starts up again, and she feels a deep tugging that makes her think of beach grass, of how you can pull and pull on it, but it never lets go.

"I'll tell you what, though, you *can* buy me a beverage this week when I take you to Cappy's for lunch. How 'bout that?"

"You're going to lunch?" Because Allison thinks she heard what she heard, but maybe she didn't.

"I go to lunch every day, silly." He reaches out and very lightly pretends to slap her face, and she does nothing. Absolutely nothing.

"Oh, Allison . . . such a serious girl." And he takes her hand and brings it to the side of his face, and she feels the pulse in his jaw, a tiny beating heart.

"Well, think about it, and tell me what day would work for you." He abruptly drops her hand.

"Thursday," she says, not thinking about it, because it's the obvious choice. She loves Thursday, which she thinks of as a complex, violet day, unlike the other days of the week, which are primary colored and lack all subtlety.

"Thursday it is. Shall I steal you away at noon?" And again Allison is shocked that he talks to her as if she decides things about her life all the time.

"My class eats at 11:25 AM." She is aware that no sophisticated lunch-taker would say this.

"That can be managed," says Rick, and he shifts in a way that makes the Jeep go back a little before it goes forward, and Allison finds this all incredibly sexy, the supervisor talk, the way the Jeep moves like it has hips.

She walks away whispering, "That can be managed, that can be managed," while simultaneously tapping into the continuous brain feed and rewinding it to the exact spot when Rick offered her a lift. And by the time she reaches the school door she has speed played every single glittering instant that followed.

—∞∞∞—

THAT NIGHT ALLISON works on her drawing of "A Woman's Mind." She is stuck on the perfect symbol for this morning's events. She tried a coffee cup, but it looked too rest-stop-sign, too Girl-Scout-badge.

She overhears her mother and Tuley talking downstairs in the kitchen about Tuley's Saturday night date. Allison can't hear everything, but Tuley comes through loud and clear every time she pounces on "gyrational." This may not be a real word. Tuley is greedy and sneaky that way; the more words she knows, the more she pretends to know.

Tuley dates a lot. Allison's mother doesn't, ever. Because her mother loved her father.

Allison's father was killed crossing a street, and her mother says about that, "Don't poke at it." Allison once heard Tuley tell a date that her father was drunk and that he was hit by a car full of drunk Boston College students. She asked Tuley whether the students went to jail. Tuley said, "Don't poke at it."

Allison hears her mother take a pass at the living room's braid rug with the electric broom, and then she begins to snap off lights, and Allison knows that's a signal that she is planning to go to bed. She can hear Tuley in her bedroom, recording words and their meanings into a tape recorder, which she'll play back while she sleeps.

There is a pause between the turning off of the front window light and the pulling of the overhead dining-room chain lamp, and Allison can tell her mother is listening all the way upstairs and hoping she'll come down and talk to her. But she won't.

"Mr. Teddy?" Allison scrambles to the window, because it's Rick's voice, and this is like a magic sign; he never calls the cat, and of course he's doing it just so he can secretly communicate with her. But then she sees that Rick is with Janie. They're in their bathrobes, waving flashlights in tiny circles toward the shrubbery, under the car, under the Jeep. Rick takes Janie's hand, and they call some more.

"Janie said Mr. Teddy has been gone since this morning," says Allison's mother. She has a habit of creeping around in her stocking feet, and already she's halfway across Allison's room. In her hand she carries a blue ceramic coffee cup with pink painted letters that read "Camille." Allison's father made it for her years ago, and it's the only one she ever uses.

It's too late for Allison to hide her sketch, and her mother curls up on the end of the bed and puts out her hand. Her at-work, pleasant, and in-charge face has almost completely given way to her at-home, tired, and wondering face. She leans toward Allison, and Allison can smell her Trésor perfume and the faint office fragrance of Xerox and pens.

"What's this a picture of, Allison?"

"A picture of thinking."

She looks at "A Woman's Mind," and turns the picture sideways, even though to Allison it's obvious the head only goes in one direction.

"Oh." And that's it. That's all her mother says about the entire catalog of her secret life. Allison is equally relieved and furious.

Rick and Janie have moved to the backyard and their calls sound weaker, yet more urgent, as if carried across water.

Allison's mother lies back on her bed. "You put so much time into a cat, and off it runs anyway," she murmurs. She's in her pre-konk-out, depressing-proclamation phase. Allison hates the dental patients on whom all her mother's niceness is spent. Her mother starts to breathe from her throat in a delicate, puzzled way that sounds as if she'll never get enough breath, never get some important question answered.

Rick and Janie stop calling Mr. Teddy, and it occurs to Allison that she was, in fact, the last person to see him. She puts her hand to the cold windowpane, where she holds it until it stings.

Allison puts her comforter over her mother, although she doesn't tuck her in, and goes downstairs to walk the different colored circles in the braid rug until exhausted, to think a Rick thought for every color, beginning with the green circle: cracked eyebrow.

THURSDAY MORNING, WHILE Allison waits for the school bus, she sees Janie standing silent and unmoving in the Wingerts' driveway. The bow of her peach silk blouse is tied in a floppy, hasty manner, and already it's slipping loose. Janie doesn't turn her head or look around. She seems preoccupied, carrying out the impossible task of measuring loss.

Just before the bus pulls up, Allison watches Janie walk to the end of the driveway and check the "Lost Cat" sign taped to the telephone pole in front of the Wingerts' house. Janie seems to read the words as if she hadn't written them herself, as if they might instead be directions to where the finding should begin.

—✺—

THERE ARE ONLY a fisherman and a woman with her elderly mother in Cappy's, but Rick takes Allison to the porch that overlooks the water. Strains of "Midnight at the Oasis" float from the kitchen. Allison thinks that she and Rick are a secret, and a secret is like carrying a pitcher of water that almost sloshes over, one she tries to keep from spilling, one she almost hopes does.

Rick removes the food from both lunch trays and sets it on a picnic table. Allison wishes she had done that. Janie would have. She moves her purse next to Rick's big black organizer. Her purse slouches over, looks like an embarrassing lavender kidney.

Allison ordered only a cup of clam chowder. Her mother has always said that when someone other than family feeds you, you wait until a specific food item is offered. But Rick said, "Whatever you want, Allison, whatever."

In the gray afternoon light, the blond in Rick's hair seems turned inside out, a flat shade of brown. He's halfway through his fried clams when he stops to gulp the orange soda he didn't let Allison buy after all. Allison doesn't usually watch grown men eat, and she's surprised at the speed with which he bites and swallows, the concentration. When her mother explained sex to her, she said it involved the man "concentrating very hard."

Rick opens his organizer and Allison gets a whiff of real leather. He turns to a certain page, taps it, continues to eat.

The wind whips her hair into one eye, and she pushes it back only to have it happen again. She takes the little blue comb from inside her purse and tries to fix her hair while staring into her lap, as if this makes the action invisible.

Rick stops eating. Then he says, "You know, Allison, you're the type of girl who will be beautiful someday, but probably not until you're thirty."

Allison looks at her chowder, which has congealed on top. Thirty. Seventeen years to wait. Might as well be nine hundred. The front of her chest feels thinned out, brittle, like a square of cold tin.

Rick says, "Allison? Allison?" He cocks his head like he's talking to a young girl. Not her.

She hears the ocean water slap stupidly, quickly against the porch pilings, as if to say, "What what what what?"

Rick closes his organizer and pushes it with some deliberation to the side of the picnic table and away from Allison's purse, which sits there foolishly, seeming to wait for the next little bit of his attention.

"But I love you now," she says. She is aware that her mouth is slipping around, that she doesn't look joyous, that people should be happy and confident when they say this thing.

"Oh, Allison." And she thinks that she sees in his eyes a certain sort of allowance, an acceptance such as a person who loves you back might have. But then something within Rick immediately pulls to the surface, something that neatly steps over whatever he might feel, and over the fact that she is crying. Her arms have gone extra dead.

"Thank you, Allison." Rick smiles at the picnic table. She is being supervised.

Then Rick asks her if she is going to eat her chowder, or she thinks he did—her listening is spotty at present, and it's not unlike being in the faulty ALM language booth at school, the one that spurts French conversations over a crackling headset. Whole sentences go missing, always the ones you really need.

Rick takes the roll that came with her soup, and he wraps it in a napkin, puts it in her purse, tells her to make sure to eat it later. He asks if she wants a cup of coffee. She shakes her head.

"Shall we, then?" he says. Now they are getting up. Getting up is the thing to do. Allison follows Rick to the wooden porch railing, all the while staring at his back. Embarrassment and longing press equally inside her heart, as if on either side of an equator. Rick puts her Styrofoam

cup of chowder on the porch railing, and a gull immediately swoops down, only to stand one inch from it, not eating, not taking.

"Ha, ha," laughs Rick.

"Ha," laughs Allison. And she's grateful, because for a
moment they are just two people laughing at a stupid bird.

Then they walk toward the stairs that lead to the
parking lot, but just before they get there Rick stops. He
seems to consider something. He takes Allison's hand and
awkwardly swings it once before he leads her behind
Cappy's kitchen to an enclosed, hidden area, where there's
nothing but a Dumpster and a jumble of wooden crates
on the ground. She doesn't understand why he puts her
in front of him with his hands on her shoulders. It seems
like he's about to calculate her height.

But instead he pulls Allison closer and very gently puts
his hands on either side of her face, and he looks at her like
a person who long ago resigned himself to a certain measure of life. No more, no less.

Then he kisses her and her insides unfurl, suddenly
beautiful, like a lush bolt of fabric thrown out upon a table.

"If you were older, you would possess me," he says, and
at that she ventures to touch him, but all she can do is gently, awkwardly, press a spot just above his right hip.

"I bet there's some boy right now who's smitten by
you," and the word *smitten* will forever mean the inside of
his mouth, the temperature of his tongue, and how he

sucks on her upper lip for just an instant, before kissing her for the second and final time of her life.

And suddenly there's light within her and light between them, a generous bestowal that spills everywhere and all at once.

Then they are simply two people, leaving a restaurant and crossing a parking lot stretched beneath plain and unending daylight.

During the drive back to school Rick says, "I have a very important meeting this afternoon." He says this too quickly, too loudly.

"What's it about?" Allison says.

"What's what about?"

"The meeting." And Rick looks puzzled for a moment, as if she'd asked a particularly personal question, and she can see that she's stepped outside a certain domain into one that now doesn't include queries about actual life activities.

"It's about benefit packages." Further questions don't seem to be expected, and Rick checks his watch, although there's a clock on the dashboard. It's 12:11, only eleven minutes past the first time Allison was truly and completely out of herself.

Just before she gets out of the car, Allison asks about Mr. Teddy.

"Still lost." Another narrowing in of all that has gone before. Rick looks down at his steering wheel. Then he looks at her and says, "Allison," and she sees one last glimpse of inexplicable yearning and confusion already corralled by guilt.

"I hope you find him soon," she says.

"I'll pass that on to Janie," says Rick.

IT'S SATURDAY MORNING, and Allison waves goodbye to her mother as she leaves for a half day of work. Her mother thanked her for this, thinking she got up early to see her off.

But Allison has a secret plan, a plan to give Rick Wingert her Pilgrim Girl picture. She stayed awake all night, polishing and rotating her memory of light until now in remembrance, it's lost all streaming capacity, is caught and hardened like a pearl.

A last push of summer sun falls across the small of Allison's back, but a cold, businesslike wind blows directly at her chest. Her body is a useless wall between two seasons.

She hunches over and stares at the Wingerts' house, willing a curtain to be drawn back, the porch light to go off. The house, unbudging, refuses to reveal anything. She traces her eyes in ever-widening circles around the home, as if it's caught in a bubble against which it threatens to burst.

Then she sees him. Mr. Teddy. He's lying motionless, stretched out on a piece of cardboard near the Wingerts' mailbox. Allison stands up, though she doesn't move, and she watches two, three, four cars drive by. It rained last night, and the road is slightly damp, as if sweating from the effort of being driven upon. She watches the road awhile longer before she looks back to the mailbox. Mr. Teddy is still there, alone.

Allison runs inside to get a towel, and she looks in the bathroom closet, but all that's left are guest towels, which are never to be used, not under any circumstance at all, and she ends up grabbing her own pink towel, which is still wet and smells of her jasmine hair conditioner.

<hr />

SOMEONE EVEN CROSSED Mr. Teddy's paws, and Allison sees no visible sign of harm until she stands over him. Then she sees that something is wrong with his mouth, which hangs open crookedly, graceless. There's so little blood for him to be dead. The air around Allison seems to tighten, and her hands feel completely weightless as they throw the towel over Mr. Teddy and bundle him up, as if he were a baby.

Allison rings the Wingerts' doorbell over and over. Its triple-tone chime sounds ridiculously, horribly happy.

Janie opens the door just a crack, already suspicious. "What is it, Allison?"

Allison looks at a little clot of face lotion that has dried near Janie's right eye.

"*What*, Allison?" And Janie pulls the collar of her robe tighter.

When she doesn't answer, Janie starts to close the door,

saying, "You're not funny, Allison, you're just not funny."

"I've got Mr. Teddy." And then Janie opens the door all the way, and she comes toward her, but Allison can't bear to put him in her arms, so instead she very gently sets him inside the house on the carpet. Janie rushes into the living room, screams for Rick, and Allison hears him running down the stairs.

The door to the Wingert home slams.

Allison turns away and starts to run. She runs like crazy, though there's no place to go. And she won't know exactly when her Pilgrim Girl picture flew from the pocket of her corduroys. But it must have, because she will never see it again, and she'll assume that it went blowing around the world, like a ticket to a place that has already been visited, of no further use to anyone.

FIVE-MINUTE HEARTS

"Ava kisses the way she walks," Matt says about his ex-wife. He speeds down the two-lane highway with no remorse, and as the afternoon light slices through passing trees, it momentarily illuminates the top of his head, creating little halos that slip off, one after the other.

Brenda remembers the way Ava walks. Those kisses must be something. She doesn't mention to Matt that, incidentally, Ava developed and refined that famous walk—a walk that contains expectant, miniature hip swoops, as if she thinks someone might at any second grab those tiny handles and kiss her crotch—circa 1983. Fenderlocken High. Brenda was there, though she doubts Ava ever noticed her.

With the car windows wide open, Matt must be going seventy, though it's hard to be sure; the broken speedometer of his '88 Volvo, "The Rocket," doesn't budge from zero. They—Matt and Brenda and Matt's four-year-old daughter, Iris—are on their way, already late, to an afternoon barbecue hosted by Ava.

———

BRENDA AND MATT met a month ago at the bookstore where Brenda works. Matt watched Brenda refuse the return of a book on which there was a faint but noticeable coffee ring. He told her he admired a woman who stood her ground. Brenda was delighted that someone would see her that way.

On their first date, Matt mentioned that his ex-wife went to the same high school as Brenda. "Sure, I knew Ava Hobbs," Brenda said in a tone of voice that would indicate she knew Ava fairly well—and didn't quite approve of her. But she'd never spoken to Ava and could barely look at Ava's feet as they passed in the school corridor.

Matt went on to say that he was in the process of changing his life, changing it for good. Brenda was impressed by such an open declaration. She herself had been in the process of changing her life for good since she was about ten.

"My bed's too small, and I fall out of it!" Iris shouts from the backseat, where, with seat belt stretched across her chest, she lurks and clutches the front seat, expelling her cheese popcorn breath in willful, ragged sighs.

Iris has two beds, one at Ava's place and one at Matt's. Brenda hasn't seen either. Brenda imagines Iris's bed at Ava's, thinks it must be covered in something with a high thread count that incorporates golden rosebuds. Her bed-cover at Matt's is probably nautical themed and hangs crookedly.

Matt scratches the inside of his right wrist, his driving wrist, the wrist that bears a navigator watch, an inscrutable timepiece, which looks like it weighs two pounds and causes his right forearm muscle to shorten under his tanned skin in a curvy, determined way. Matt told Brenda that he used to be a big drinker. He says Ava used to be a big drinker, too. Apparently they were such big drinkers they had to keep a case of Pedialyte in the fridge for hangovers. But those days are gone. Matt even has a new job. He sells a software program to California sheriffs that helps them keep track of criminals.

"Which bed, honey?" Matt says and reaches behind his seat to squeeze Iris's ankle.

Brenda turns completely around to listen to Iris's answer, unlike a real mother. She thinks of the board game Life that she played as a child ("Spin the wheel of fate, then drive the hilarious game path of fortune!"). Brenda recalls loading her tiny car with kids the size of rice and driving as fast as possible around a cardboard square.

Iris flops against the backseat. "My bed at school!"

Iris goes to two different day-care centers, one when she's at Matt's place, one when she's at Ava's. Ava works at a beauty supply store six days a week; Matt also works Saturdays. The only thing upon which Matt and Ava are united is to call day care "school." Brenda has overheard them talking on Matt's cell phone. "When she gets out of school . . . today at school . . ." Iris has been in school since she was six months old.

Brenda never went to day care, doesn't know anyone who did. It wasn't invented yet. She does remember kindergarten, and there certainly weren't beds. There was the laying of one's head on one's hands at a long wooden table, which smelled of grape juice and Cheez Whiz. And there was the listening to fingers tapping, jawbones clunking, and bang-plastered foreheads thudding all the way down the line, sounds that occur when one asks oneself "What Will I Be When I Grow Up?"—or that's what Mrs. Gosseltaff would tell you all that racket was, for she often urged her pupils to "give it some thought" while resting. But Mrs. Gosseltaff's students, each of them in that terrible, alone-forever, face-to-table position, weren't thinking at all about jobs, for they were beating out with tiny skulls and hand bones, the *other* big question, the bigger big question: Who will I love?

Who will I love?

The inside of The Rocket is now the temperature of

a meat locker, and Brenda asks Matt, who has the window controls, to put hers up.

"What?" he asks.

"People like Brenda make the air cold!" Iris shrieks, and this Matt does seem to hear, since he immediately puts up his daughter's window.

Brenda figures she'll tough it out. "Iris, do you want to try your coloring book?" The velveteen-covered mythological coloring book, an item for which she paid too much, even with her employee discount, has been shoved off to the side of the backseat, open to a picture of a minotaur whose right horn is covered in a fine layer of orange popcorn dust.

"Do you like the minotaur?" Brenda asks Iris, who pulls at her pale red eyebrows and stares at her lap. "The minotaur was half man and half bull," says Brenda.

"Who's the fool?" demands Iris with all the conviction of a hard-boiled DA.

A chunk of hair blows into Brenda's mouth, hair she cut only last week. She pulls the tangled lock out of her mouth. "Why are you asking about a fool, Iris?"

"You said, 'half man, half fool.'" A motorcycle with a broken muffler passes their car.

"I didn't say that, Iris!" shouts Brenda.

Matt glances at his watch, assessing his heart—its rapidity. Brenda had never seen such a watch before she saw Matt's. She doesn't wear a watch herself. Matt accelerates and The Rocket makes a startling, heart-wrenching noise like a woman crying in her sleep.

"Hold on to your dental work, ladies!" yells Matt as the front end of The Rocket visibly begins to shake.

Brenda wants to tell Matt to knock it off and slow down, but she feels she doesn't know him well enough, and now, due to her infallible politeness, they may all lose their lives. Her hair whips every which way, and she attempts to aim her head in the right direction, the direction that might make it stop, but no such luck, and it occurs to her that she doesn't even have a comb in her purse, and that when she sees Ava in as soon as fifteen minutes from now, and for the first time in eighteen years, she'll look like a total wreck.

A truck the deep black color of charred firewood is overtaking them, and it's unclear why the driver, whose face can't be seen through his window, is going so fast. And why does he need to race Matt and Brenda and Iris in their poor old Volvo—this mocked-up, thrown-together example of a family such as never navigated the Life board—as they speed toward Ava and her amazing walk?

"Who's the fool? Who's the fool?" Iris keeps on.

The truck, upon them now, honks, or more accurately bellows, like an animal about to charge.

Matt, Brenda, Iris, and their new friend, Del Stanger, are on the side of a barren shoulder just off the 170 in Van Nuys. Del, in his big black truck, witnessed them veer off the road as a multitude of tiny rocks flew up under the car, clattering like finger bones. The first thing he said to them was, "Everyone's lucky sometimes."

Iris pretends to wash the pavement with her hair.

"Get up, Iris," says Matt as he and Del Stanger assess the damage to the blown back-right tire.

"I want candy," says Iris, and she does lift her head, but not high enough to keep the end of her red ponytail from dragging in the dust.

"Stop this behavior within five, Iris," says Matt.

Del flops down on the embankment, as if he's glad to be in the dirt, and puts his hands up into the wheel well. Matt, who never works on his own car, stands to the side of the passenger door with his hands on his hips. Del makes an unself-conscious kind of grunt, and Brenda notices the strong bones of his face. Long black hair escapes from a baseball cap that reads *Trail,* and it's probably just the brand name of some product that Del once lugged coast to coast, but Brenda finds this romantic. She imagines Del driving in a remote area just before nightfall, thinks of him sitting in the cab of his truck, very alone and overwhelmed by the beauties and mysteries that hourly pass his window. Truckers are unrealized poets, she thinks. Who else would sit in one place, day after day, talking to no one, watching everything, traveling the same piece of life's road, forward and back?

"Thank you for trying to stop us," says Brenda. No comment from beneath the car. "And it's exceptionally nice of you to help with the tire," Brenda adds, too formal to her own ears.

Brenda and Matt stand apart from each other, both staring at the lower half of Del's body, which reveals a tan line between his jeans and T-shirt. Now Brenda has her hands on her hips, too. Cars pass, people look at the dumpy green Volvo stopped at a crazy angle. Some of them slow, none of them stop.

"I want candy," repeats Iris, and she stands up, seemingly aware that exactly five minutes have passed. Brenda fishes for a Lifesaver in her purse.

"*Why* do you want candy, Iris?" asks Matt. "Give me one abstract reason."

Matt says he likes to make Iris's brain work. He's helping her create paths. He read an article about it in the parenting section of his electronic record storage professionals' magazine. This kind of thing makes Brenda's skin crawl, this overworking of matters. And in that instant Brenda knows that she and Matt aren't a fit. Immediately she feels a sort of internal sliding over the fact.

"Because I like candy," Iris answers after great deliberation.

"That's a concrete reason, honey," says Matt.

"It is?" Brenda says.

The bookstore where Brenda works was recently voted "The Expensive Person's Bookstore" in the local hipster's weekly, although the book prices, set by publishers, are the same as everywhere else. Brenda and her underpaid coworkers are the type who read Proust for kicks, who crack each other up with subtle jokes that encase the obscure fact, the scrap of unusable knowledge. Since the newspaper article, they've begun to make comments like "*That's* an expensive statement." Most, like Brenda, would hope to seem smart and funny, though they're all riddled with sensitivities and quirks, the oddness of which they try to mitigate through enlargement.

Everyone teases Brenda about her lack of a watch and *great* disinterest in time, which she exaggerates for the sake of a joke and to lessen the fact that she desperately worries about her hours and days, the fact that they are slipping by so easily and still, true love has not been found.

"Well, the wheel rim is all right, and I thought your axle was tweaked, but it's not."

Del stretches a long leg out from under the car and rocks his head side to side. No one has ever looked so comfortable on the earth.

"So?" says Matt.

"So, you need a tire." Del offers to take Matt up the road to get one, and Matt questions Brenda and Iris's safety.

"Don't worry," says Del. "Mostly canine breeders in these parts. People here would sooner kill you over your dog than your wife."

"That's not my wife," says Matt as he checks his back pocket for his wallet.

Del looks at Brenda, seems to really look at her for the first time, and an expression crosses his face, as if he's remembered something, and again Brenda imagines that his thoughts are rich and deep, and she suddenly wishes she could know him.

"Thank you, again," she says and extends her hand.

Iris throws herself around his knees. To the Lexus-load of businessmen passing at this instant, Iris and Brenda and Del might look like a family saying goodbye to one another.

"You'll be okay with Iris?" Matt asks Brenda as he steps closer to her and clamps his arm around her, pinning her to him. Brenda knows that Matt will later give Iris some complicated lecture about how you can't just give your heart to a stranger because he shows up in your life for five minutes.

The men drive away in the black truck, and Brenda and Iris stand there, looking at each other. For once Iris is absolutely still. "Let's sit down, Iris," says Brenda, and immediately Iris does, too hard, right on the pavement. She even folds her hands, and this seems like something she was told to do in day care, and it occurs to Brenda how stressful it is to be a child, with everyone telling you what to do, what to want, trying to create trails in your head every other minute.

Iris starts to yawn, or it looks like a yawn, but it suddenly and vociferously mutates into crying, and this crying has a rhythm to it: sob hard, no breathing, then wait—sob hard, no breathing, then wait. This crying is more like questioning, though Brenda doesn't know what Iris is asking. It seems like asking.

And what would Ava do? But all Brenda can imagine is a girl walking away from her down a hallway, the cold hallway, the one outside the gym, where the exit door was always propped open to blow away sweat, a girl with an arm lined with silver bracelets, a girl with a walk like no other girl on earth, the exact girl that Brenda would have been, if she could have been any other girl.

MATT HAD TOLD Brenda that Ava lived in a typical California condo and Brenda pictured a Mexican-tiled entryway, a courtyard with calla lilies and freesia. She hadn't expected the single-story units all in need of paint, the smell of Pine Sol, cigarettes, and, everywhere, burnt teriyaki chicken.

Everyone here looks like they could use a little help.

Two young men box dangerously close to a hibachi. An older man, wearing a leather vest over his bare chest, sits across a picnic table from a woman whose peach-colored hair matches her lipstick and nails. They both look a few beers in. Between them are three snack bowls, all of them empty. It's five o'clock, and the sky, a rinse water blue, is lined with stretched-thin clouds that look like so much illegible handwriting.

Looking up at Matt and Brenda, the woman says, "Sherry Taylor," vehemently, as if someone had disputed her name. "My Pete," she says, waving a long orange fingernail at the man. Pete nods at the two shirtless boxers and says, "Dale," then "Pixie." Dale wears high white knee socks and long green shorts that hang low on his hips. Pixie ties a yellow bandana around his head. The two begin to circle each other.

"Family business," Sherry says without looking at Matt or Brenda.

"Fighting?" Brenda asks.

"Boxing," Sherry indignantly corrects her.

There are no other guests. This is Ava's barbecue? Where is Ava?

Matt, holding Iris's hand in his left, nervously flexes his right arm, his navigating arm. Last week he bought a two-hundred-dollar electric stimulus box to work his muscles. Brenda lay in her bed—Matt had spent the night—watching him attach all those electrodes; it took some doing. But Matt is committed.

Brenda spots Ava sitting in a lawn chair on an unprosperous patch of lawn. She smokes with one hand and holds a conch shell ashtray in the other, though she flicks her ashes onto the beat-up grass. Her back is to Matt and his troupe as they cross the lawn, and she is hunched over, as if she were watching late-night TV—a way that no one would sit if they thought anyone were watching.

Iris runs toward Ava's chair and Ava, as if she feels a sudden burst of sun upon her back, turns around. But Iris stops halfway across the scrubby courtyard, fascinated by the boxers. Ava gives Brenda a "what can you expect?" look, and Brenda thinks she sees a flash of recognition in Ava's still wide, still beautiful green eyes. Brenda feels a small surge of pride at being able to look directly at her.

Then Ava smiles, and Brenda notices how yellow her teeth are. They were never like that. And somehow, Ava is so very pulled in upon herself. When she stands up she seems shorter than Brenda remembered. "I thought you weren't coming," she says to Matt, and her words seem loose inside her mouth. Matt mentions the blown tire as he turns his body sideways to hug her. Ava starts coughing violently. They look like two people at the end of a dinner party that didn't go so well.

"I guess you remember Brenda," says Matt, looking at his navigator watch instead of either woman's face.

"You guess?" Brenda says, trying for a joke and an appearance of offhand confidence.

Ava nods and smokes, but Brenda can tell Ava has no idea what he's talking about. Matt might as well have said, "Would you agree that Brenda has a head?"

Ava fixates on the last half inch of her cigarette. Her hair, once thick and glossy, has been curled at the ends, but sections have been missed, and some lie absolutely straight between the waves. Ava runs her fingers through her locks, and Brenda notices how red and angry her nail beds are. She remembers a thing she once heard about Ava, a thing she forgot because she couldn't believe it.

Halfway through Brenda's junior year at Fenderlocken High, Ava had disappeared. A rumor circulated that she'd left to go to a fashion institute in San Francisco. Perhaps she was studying to be a designer. Of course she would be accepted at sixteen. She was Ava.

Brice Manelli told Brenda that Ava actually had gone to "sewing school," which was something completely different, a young women's halfway house that sheltered girls with drug, drinking, and behavioral problems, as well as indistinct or compound problems that no one could quite unravel. Brenda didn't believe any of this. What problems could Ava have?

Brice said, "Well, all I know is that I sat next to her in Home Ec, and she spent the whole time sticking pins and needles under her fingernails. And you know what she said when I asked her about it? She said, 'It always heals.'"

But of course Brenda hadn't believed that either.

———

DALE DANCES AROUND Pixie, who has pulled the yellow bandana from his head and wrapped it around his upper arm like a tourniquet. They stare into each other's eyes as if mesmerized. Then Pixie springs at Dale and takes a swipe, hitting him squarely in his right rib.

"That's it," Sherry Taylor calls.

Once again, Ava starts hacking, this time before she gets a chance to cover her mouth.

From his plastic lawn chair, Matt says, "Have another cigarette, why don't you." Ava stiffens. The air seems to quicken and gather between them. Matt starts to ask something, then stops, sighs.

"Because I'm too high-strung," Ava says, seemingly joyless at her ability to know what he would have asked.

"More like lazy." And this is where it starts. It's as if there was a blue flash in the air, and even Sherry and Pete shift their attention to Ava and Matt. In one of the condominiums someone puts on music, an old speed-metal song, and Iris immediately starts spinning to this tune that has no discernable melody or rhythm.

"Why can't you stop smoking?" Matt says. "I just want to know," he adds, as he glances at Brenda, then folds his arms across his chest, affecting the stance of a reasonable man.

"Why do you bring a different woman to my home every month?" says Ava, gesturing toward her front stoop. It features a penicillin-pink door behind a slab of cement littered with pizza flyers. She attempts to light another cigarette. "I just want to know."

Brenda walks over to the empty snack bowls. Just last week Matt told her she was the first woman he'd dated since his divorce eight months ago.

"This is about smoking," Matt says to Ava in a tone that one would use on an unruly child in church.

"This is *not* about smoking."

"Besides, you've been drinking."

"I've not been drinking."

"Well, you're on *something.*"

"I am not." Ava gestures wildly with her cigarette, as if to poke holes in the sky.

"Then why are you acting this way?"

"What way?" Ava chews at a cuticle. "What way?" she repeats.

Matt's face shows no emotion. He could be a man waiting at a stoplight.

"Oh, am I embarrassing you in front of your new friend?" Ava does a little rocking step back and forth.

"Stop it, Ava."

"Stop it yourself, you box."

"Oh, I'm a box."

"You're a box, " and here Ava's voice cracks, "and you have no understanding about real people who feel real things, people who've been through a thing or two and know something about the accordion of life on down!"

Iris twirls past them.

Then simply, as if their past life together has suddenly come unzipped, Matt and Ava's entire history of disagreements tumbles out. Words flash and spin in the air: *Liar, wrong, can, don't, you, fuck, mine, care, stop, always, you, why, shouldn't, try, you, said, why, didn't, help, me, you, you, you.* Matt and Ava stand absolutely still. At this moment they look curiously formal and attentive and, in some small way, in love.

Iris spins faster and faster.

Ava tries for one last drag. Matt reaches for her forearm, which is pale and bears not a single silver bracelet. Someone turns up the ugly music, which seems to rip sideways on itself and sounds impossibly tangled. Iris spins so hard she falls on the ground. She does not cry. Matt, still holding on to Ava's forearm, shouts for her to drop the cigarette. Dale and Pixie stop boxing.

"I said, drop it!" With arms lifted, Matt and Ava are frozen for a moment, a statue of furious unity. Then Ava bites Matt's wrist. His navigating wrist. A vein in her forehead sticks out. Ava, the beautiful.

Matt falls down on one knee as if she'd bitten his leg. Ava stands with her hands covering her face. Brenda runs to Matt and puts one palm on his shoulder, but he pulls away from her. The mystery DJ has turned down the music, but not all the way, and Brenda can hear a tiny scrap of bass that urgently repeats, sounding like a fly caught against a screen. Tap, tap—tap, tap.

Sherry and Pete and their sons huddle around Matt. Sherry quite practically asks if there's blood. Considering her family business, this must be small potatoes. Pixie gives Matt his yellow bandana. Pete, with his hands on his thighs, leans into Matt, speaking quietly and directly, saying something that no one can hear. Ringside, there's always some fellow like this. Matt gives his complete and utter attention to this man with whom he's not previously exchanged two words.

Brenda sits in the lawn chair that Ava earlier vacated. Iris runs to her side, flushed from spinning. "I've got a bed here," she says matter-of-factly. Brenda tries to pull Iris onto her lap, and Iris does allow this, but once there she swings her feet sideways and sits quite straight. She might as well be taking a seat on a bus. Iris will be held, but she won't be comforted.

Ava hasn't moved from the spot where she bit Matt. She absently wipes her mouth with the back of her hand. Then, without taking one look at Matt or Brenda or Iris, she goes to the picnic table, picks up the three empty snack bowls, and with great finality stacks them one inside the other. She turns and heads toward her front door. The way she walks, she could be shoveling dirt.

WHATEVER IT IS that Pete said to Matt causes him to jump up and follow Ava. He still holds the bandana around his wrist, and as an afterthought he calls to Iris, who runs to him. Brenda trails after, but Matt and Iris are already behind the closed pink door before she's halfway across the lawn. She turns around and almost bumps into Pete and his sons. Pixie smiles, though Dale and Pete give her a look as if they've never seen her before. Brenda stands in the middle of the yard for a few moments, completely directionless.

Finally Sherry Taylor waves Brenda over to the picnic table. "My Pete knows what's what," she declares as Brenda joins her. Brenda nods and Sherry adds, "The first time we slept together that man spit on my face to see what I really looked like."

"That's something," Brenda answers, but what she's really listening to is a sound coming from behind the pink door. Iris is singing a nonsense song, and much of it is unclear except the part she keeps repeating about a man and a fool.

"Because in those days, I just lathered on the makeup."

"Sure," Brenda answers. Behind Sherry, Brenda sees Ava and Matt framed in Ava's kitchen window. She cranes her neck to get a better view.

"My Pete believes in the reality of passion." Sherry Taylor taps her fingernails against an empty beer can, and it is clear she expects something from Brenda.

"He must be very passionate."

Sherry Taylor giggles wickedly.

Through the kitchen window Brenda sees Matt hold up his forearm, watches Ava wrap his wrist in gauze. Then she cuts the gauze with scissors—huge scissors, the wrong scissors. Matt lets her do it anyway. The trust.

Matt disappears from the window and Brenda sees Ava standing there alone, head tilted in an old familiar way, a way that in high school had seemed proud and arrogant but now looks resigned. And free of something, too. Ava has quit her own beauty, the whole complex freight of it. But for a moment Brenda can still see it, almost see it, now more like a ring around her, something vaporous, something vanishing.

Matt pokes his head out the door and shouts, "Brenda, I'm calling you a taxi. Okay? Okay?" Just like that. Brenda doesn't give him an answer, and he doesn't wait for one.

Sherry Taylor looks at Brenda and gently asks, "What do you *do,* Brenda?"

For an instant, it seems to Brenda that she's inquiring into her past line of relationship errors, or perhaps what she will do in the future to avoid them.

"I work at a bookstore."

"Oh, I like bookstores. So nice and quiet." Sherry winks at her, as if she understands something further about bookstore work, something impractical or silly.

It would be closing hour now. Time for easing out the last customer of the day. Time to pick up the book left carelessly on the floor, splayed open, aisles from its proper home.

Sherry says, "The great thing about the book business is that people will always need to read. Just like my business. Just like boxing."

———

AFTER SHERRY TAYLOR leaves, Brenda sits at the picnic table, waiting for her taxi. The smells of chicken, Pine Sol, and cigarettes have at last lifted, and now there is only cold night air to breathe. Brenda looks up at the darkening sky, at the fast clouds charging by, clouds that in moments will be in the next town, or the one after that. She thinks of Del Stanger, imagines him driving his black truck around the world, seeing beauty at every turn. Where is he now?

Then Brenda recalls something else about Life, a thing she hadn't thought of in years, about how everyone tried to avoid the "Flat Tire Miss Next Turn" square. Because while one's car was stuck, the rest of the players whizzed on by, collecting with the roll of the dice all sorts of things—jobs, marriage, kids. But of course, everything was random, everything could be lost, and none of it had to do with love.

UNSTRUCK

JULIE AND HER temporary brother, Pritchard, had been getting married every single day since they'd heard that maybe a family had been found for Pritchard, since school got called off for a week due to snow, since Julie's mother insisted every afternoon that they eat four to six orange halves, which they did, sucking out the juicy flesh, grinding their teeth against orange peel until their lips were on fire and they had burning red mouth shadows.

"Kids?" Julie's mother shouted from upstairs in the kitchen. "What are you doing?"

No answer from the basement. Julie and Pritchard were busy having a touching tongues contest. Besides, Julie's mother worked as a part-time channeler. She channeled a dead man from Sussex, England, named Mr. Darlton. If she wanted to know what they were doing, she could go ask him.

Pritchard broke first. "I'm stinging. I'm dying. Fix me," he said to Julie. Pritchard was supposedly eleven. Julie was actually eleven. She sat across from him wrapped in the happy house afghan that her mother had crocheted for her birthday. Chartreuse, yellow, and lavender, every house was chock-full of holes.

"Sometimes I take my clothes off because it's a nice thing to do," said Julie.

Snow could make a person feel reckless! The not seeing out. The no one seeing in. Newscasters blathering about bread and milk, and Get Some Now. The packed, stuffy safety of it all, while outside the snow fell one flake at a time until its big fat beauty threatened to crush everything in sight.

Yesterday, Julie had heard her mother say the stripping thing while she was on the phone with Julie's father. Her mother was scrubbing a pan with a Brillo pad, but she said this as if she'd just woken up. Julie's mother, though slender, often complained of feeling heavy—not overweight, just heavy. The previous month she had her skeleton weighed in a special experiment at MIT for large-boned people. Eighty-eight pounds. Sometimes she just stared at her forearms on the kitchen table, calculating.

"Julie, fix me," Pritchard said, rolling on the brand-new green and orange Fiesta Time indoor/outdoor rug. The salesman told Julie's parents that the rug was made with "wonder-weave" technology. Wonder-weave was wondrous! It could even be hosed down. Pritchard scratched his neck against it like a dog. Pritchard's hair smelled of dirt, chicken, grease, and wind. His eyes were a strange flat green like the back of a leaf. His mouth was too large for his face, and his puffy lower lip was creased in the middle as if it had once been folded in half. It was rumored that Pritchard was actually twelve. Once Pritchard told Julie he was thirteen. But then he took it back.

The Windbreaker that Pritchard wore (nonstop and zipped to his chin) featured over his heart one green wave and one blue wave that rose in tandem, touching each other, about to break at any second. A little white penguin was sewn where the tips of the waves met. Since he'd been with Julie's family, Pritchard wore the Windbreaker to school each day, and Julie's mother let him.

The Baimas, Pritchard's second temporary family, had given him this jacket. Pritchard was always bragging about how the Baimas bought the Windbreaker at a big famous clothing outlet, and how they'd given him money to buy his own food since he was eight. He used to eat at McDonald's every single meal, like a superstar.

Pritchard was already in trouble at school. On the top of every piece of homework he passed in, on his drawings in art class, on his desk, and all over his hands he wrote: *I Love My Wife Julie.* This was inappropriate, his teacher had said. It suggested confusion within generally accepted family member roles. Julie heard her father read the letter sent from school to her mother. Still, this didn't stop Pritchard and her from getting married every day.

Before Pritchard, Julie was not feared or admired at school. She was a quiet person leaning against a wall somewhere waiting to go to the next thing. But now she was Pritchard's Sister—Pritchard who pushed down the hallway as if he were a man running through a wild meadow, a man about to jump aboard his own private helicopter, a man who shoved the other kids into their minilockers, muttering cryptic warnings such as: "Wish you didn't, didn't, huh? Too late. Too late. Cry. Or run." It wasn't like he was swearing, and he sometimes smiled when he said these things. Julie's mother had been called to school, though.

"Are you saying you want to discipline him for accusing people of regret?" she said to the principal. Julie's mother had a thing about regret. She called it "the useless emotion."

The principal admitted that Julie's mother had a point. He said this was just part of the school's new Stay Alert, No One Gets Hurt campaign. Just a little warning, he said to Julie's mother. No big deal.

That first night at Julie's house Pritchard refused to eat. He said he'd already been to McDonald's three times that day. Julie's father said, "Don't worry, pal, we're the type of folks who only eat when we're hungry."

"Right," said Pritchard.

Such a tough, glamorous response, Julie thought. If only she could talk that way.

"So, Pritchard, what kinds of things excite you? What are your passions?" Julie's father was a drama teacher at a private girls' school. Apparently this was how girls liked to be talked to, even though he never asked Julie any questions like that. Julie could tell that Pritchard made her father nervous—the way Pritchard sat tipped at a forty-five-degree angle on the back legs of his kitchen chair, not answering, gripping the arms as if he might launch into outer space at any second. Then there was the wetness of his lower lip, and how a perfect bead of saliva collected in the tiny valley at its center.

Finally Julie's father said, "Well, Pritchard, although we may take a little getting used to, we're just regular folks, and we want you to know that while a family is being found for you, you are part of—"

"The earth has more than one moon," Pritchard cut him off, and a little bit of spit flew from his mouth. "In 1986, scientists found Corinthe, the baby moon. The baby moon is three miles wide with a horseshoe-shaped orbit that lasts seven hundred and seventy years."

"There you go," said Julie's father.

"It's just as good as the first moon," Pritchard said.

After dinner Julie followed Pritchard into his bedroom/canned goods/extra box room. He took his unpacked Safari Boy suitcase off the bed and lifted it up and down a few times. Pritchard said he could pack the suitcase in such a way that it weighed absolutely nothing. He showed Julie how you had to tuck everything into the side pockets and put no items in the middle. The agency people would check for weight. Pritchard also told Julie you could tell an agency lady by the blouse covered in hopping birdies or the bright sweater with a big cat brooch. The men wore sickeningly happy ties. "It's a rule or some such," Pritchard said. "Some such." No one Julie knew used that phrase, and the way he said it with the two words carelessly exhaled, like he was smoking them, was almost more than Julie could stand.

"Do you kids want one last orange half?" Julie's mother called down the stairs. "Or you may have *one* real fruit Popsicle." The garage refrigerator/freezer, which sat just outside the basement door like a squat yellow guest too shy to ever knock, was packed tight with boxes of real fruit Popsicles made of sixty-five percent real fruit chunks.

"But don't you *dare* go out there in your bare feet. There could be melted snow out there! You could be grounded!" she shouted. Julie's mother constantly reminded them that when they were in the garage they should *never* touch the refrigerator/freezer door when they took their boots off after playing in the snow, because the garage floor could be wet, and then they'd get grounded, and they'd be stuck forever to the refrigerator/freezer, and all the thoughts in their heads would be shaken to pieces and never come together in the right way again. "If you get grounded, you can't let go no matter how hard you try," she had cautioned. "And if anyone tries to save you, they won't be able to let go of you either."

"Julie, fix me, fix me, fix me," chanted Pritchard. Fixing always led to marriage.

Not touching his red-hot mouth shadows, Julie put her fingers on either side of his lips and they squeezed open, and this was how it happened the first time—it was a treatment to fix a burning mouth. But Pritchard would leave his mouth open way past shutting time, his too-big mouth with his slick lower lip, and this was always part of the treatment/accident/marriage. Then Julie would open hers, and get up very close to him and breathe into him, pretending this was her last breath on earth. She would give it to Pritchard, and he would hold it.

Today, after thirty seconds, Pritchard's eyes began to tear up. "Let it out, your heart will burst," Julie commanded. The white penguin pitched into the sea of Pritchard's jacket and drowned. Pritchard clamped his arms to his stomach, fighting to keep her air inside him.

"I've got someone coming in half an hour, you kids," Julie's mother called. A client, Julie thought. Not even a snowstorm could keep them away. "So I want you to shovel then." Julie's mother needed great privacy to properly make contact with Mr. Darlton.

Before he died, Mr. Darlton had been a merchant who imported Indian textiles to England, and he now came as a messenger to help people whose hearts had been trammeled.

Once a man had come to their house who'd been drinking from a broken heart, and generally Julie's mother didn't accept that sort of thing, but this time she said if the man would sit down at the kitchen table and eat a little something, she'd channel while he sobered up. No sooner did she make contact with Mr. Darlton than the man decided to rest his head in his plate of pasta. Julie's mother murmured that he really shouldn't be so discouraged over his love life because there was, at that very moment, a special word coming through from Mr. Darlton.

"Anaharta," she whispered, then paused. Obviously it was the type of word that needed no other words around it because it meant so much. Apparently Mr. Darlton picked up this word in India. Everyone in India, even little kids, knew it meant the unstruck heart. The unstruck heart was one that could never be hurt for good.

Pritchard still held his breath. He stared out the window, concentrating on the sun, which just now looked like the tip of a finger pushed through a dark blue afternoon sky. The sky was brooding, about to snow again. Later that afternoon a solar eclipse was to occur. The moon was going to swell up and roll in front of the sun. The sun would go out, then suddenly it would reappear. They'd been told at school not to look directly at any of this. Not even if there were clouds covering the sun, because the clouds could suddenly part, and if that happened, they'd been told: STOP LOOKING IMMEDIATELY!

Already Pritchard was looking. Still, he wasn't breathing. Upstairs they heard Julie's mother drop the cast-iron pan on the stove. Maybe she was going to make them fried chicken because they'd been so good at eating oranges.

Pritchard and Julie weren't going to let anyone take him away, no matter what. They would control this with their brains. Originally, Pritchard was supposed to stay with Julie's family for "just a little while," but it had turned into five months. The agency hadn't found a family for him until just last week. Pritchard said it sometimes took three or four years to really check a family out, and by that time he and Julie could be living in their very own dream home. Julie had felt a pinch of disbelief in her chest, but she didn't let on.

Julie watched Pritchard struggle not to breathe, watched a place in the front of his neck suddenly pop out as if there were a tiny hand inside. She thought about how the previous night Pritchard had told her that they could get jobs as dishwashers at the International House of Pancakes so they could save up for their dream home. Pritchard knew an older kid who would get them in. The kid said that lots of children worked there; nobody minded. Pritchard had said the Baimas lived next door to the International House of Pancakes, and that if he asked them, they would probably let Julie and him sleep in their garage during the week. That way they could get to work in less than ten seconds and really impress the bosses.

Pritchard made a small abrupt sound inside himself like something had been knocked off a shelf. He was turning the color of a bruised peach.

There had been something else about the Baimas. Pritchard told Julie they were Jehovah's Witnesses, and that in exchange for sleeping in their garage, all he and Julie would probably have to do is walk around with the Baimas one day a week and tell people things like, "In 1914, Satan was kicked out of heaven with the rest of the demons." Pritchard had done it plenty when he lived with them, and he said it was fun. People always wanted to know the whole story—why 1914? What happened to Satan then? Where did the demons live after that? It could take all afternoon to explain these things. Sometimes people brought out snacks. Pritchard had been allowed to sit quietly on the sofa and fall asleep if he wanted. He wasn't to offer any comments about Satan. And he definitely wasn't supposed to mention anything about the demonized sofa in the Baimas' living room, and how they got the demon out by yelling, "Jehovah! Jehovah!" really, really loud.

Upstairs, oil was starting to spit in the frying pan, and Julie imagined her mother with her long chicken-cooking fork, jumping at the chicken, quickly stabbing it and flipping it. She simply had no use for spatter screens. "You can't let fear rule your life," she would say.

At last Pritchard exhaled, and his breath sounded like a small bus pulling into a station. "Fifty-four seconds," he said. The higher the number, the more he loved her.

"Fifty-four," she repeated. Chicken smoke trailed downstairs.

Pritchard had a certain look in his eyes. Julie could see it coming.

Pritchard grabbed Julie and pushed her on the floor facedown. He lay on top of her, and she could feel his heart beating into her back. He locked his calves around her ankles. "Do you like me? Do you love me? Or what?"

A snowplow started down the street, the second one that hour. The plow dragged its scraper along the street, hungry for snow. Julie couldn't breathe.

Pritchard pushed his forehead into the back of her neck. His Windbreaker was sliding around, and some of it had bunched up on one side. "It's *love me,* right? Love me, right?" and he sounded scared, like he was running toward something and trying to get away, at the same time. From behind her he kissed her right cheek hard and in the same place over and over. Now Julie was breathing. She was breathing the rug. And once she kissed it. And at that moment she thought of Pritchard as not smelling of dirt, chicken, grease, and wind, but like the Fiesta Time rug, which smelled like new rubber bands and the tissue inside shoe boxes times ten, and that was just one of the wonders of wonder-weave. Wonder-weave, wonder-weave. Pritchard and Julie were a wonder-weave. Now *this* was being married! Pritchard tried to drop into Julie's mouth from the side. Julie reached back and pinched the dent in the bottom of his neck. Pritchard grabbed Julie's hand and bit at her thumbnail. Julie pushed against the rug like a lady holding up a building. Still Pritchard was able to pull up her shirt. From behind he pressed her right nipple like an elevator button that wasn't working. Julie's breath stopped again, stopped in a funny way, and crouched somewhere against her back. Pritchard was crying a little and saying *please.* His big front teeth scraped the back of her skull. Please, please. Pritchard was a dog head, pushing. Pritchard was a man whose head had fallen in a plate. They were pressing hard together, getting nowhere, doing nothing, being married.

The smoke alarm went off. The entire house smelled like burnt chicken. Julie's mother turned on the radio loud to try to cover up the fact.

"WKBL the Paaaarrty Station!" Now her mother was dancing to the classic disco station, stamping her big heavy-boned feet. She was trying not to regret the chicken.

From where Julie and Pritchard lay on the floor, they could see the snow pile up against the window. The sun looked so tiny and pale now. Pritchard looked out, staring at it harder than ever. How could the sun hurt you just for looking at it?

———∞———

JULIE DOUBLE-TIED her snow boot laces for luck as she always did. Pritchard left his undone, and they flapped around like two small hapless arms as he stepped out into the garage. He didn't bother to flip the light switch. They weren't little babies. To the side of the door the yellow refrigerator/freezer sat humming its electrical anthem, cheery against all odds. It seemed to glow and appeared larger than usual—a sun that had eaten the moon whole. Even though their feet weren't wet, even though they wore boots, even though there was absolutely no chance of getting grounded, they kept their distance.

They took their twin snow shovels—which had been purchased at Sears, and weren't just kids' shovels but real small adult ones—and they stepped out into the cold.

Everything was covered in snow with the same equal and unabiding love. The lawn, the trees, the toolshed, the telephone pole, all seemed far more dignified than just the day before. It was the same old world, but better. Julie and Pritchard walked the few feet that Julie's father had shoveled that morning and then lifted themselves up and over into the deeper snow, where they stood unmoving. For a moment it was too beautiful to break up and smash with their stomping. They were the only two on earth, it seemed.

Then came the crank and rumble of a snowplow and the

eerie sound of machinery dropping, or maybe it was lifting, but it was like a woman singing. A woman with a cold.

"That's an E," said Pritchard, and he started to spin like mad, his arms straight out to the side. In less than one minute he would be in Funny Time. Funny Time was the whole world whooshing in big bright glimpses past a person's head. Funny Time was a chance to see things for the first and last time ever—again and again and again. Funny Time was a strange up-thrown feeling in the stomach, just like love. Pritchard had taught it to Julie, and now she started to spin too. The yard was flipping by them in its huge white glory. Roof tips were jagging. The sky held fast. Julie and Pritchard were wild with joy in their happy, tilting world.

Then there was a man coming up the driveway. They saw—saw—saw him from the corners of their eyes. A man—a man—a man swirl. A black coat. A flying head. A man. Right there in the middle of Pritchard and Julie's Funny Time.

The man looked at Pritchard and Julie, then just at Pritchard. Pritchard looked at the man. The man looked at the sky. "Don't look at the sun," Pritchard said under his breath, and he lifted his shovel to his shoulder like a gun.

"Don't shoot," said the man, and he patted his gloved hand over his heart in a theatrical way, in a way that looked like nothing so much as where a person should aim. The man wore a dark coat with a high collar that snapped. Around the collar a paisley silk scarf was tied in a complicated way. No one Pritchard or Julie knew wore such a thing. And certainly not in winter. He looked like a man from another time.

"Mr. Darlton?" Julie called, because even though Mr. Darlton was supposedly dead, maybe he wasn't, maybe he just lived across town.

The man started walking toward them again. He wasn't smiling. He carried a black bag. He did not swing it. No sickeningly happy tie was visible. He walked the purposeful walk of someone who gives you a shot. Someone just doing his job, even when that job is to hurt you. He never took his eyes off Pritchard. He was a helpful man come to help. Anyone could tell.

Pritchard zagged left to the side of the yard. He was elbowing needlessly. He zagged right. He ran in a circle around himself. "Wish you didn't, didn't, huh?" he shouted. In the blank white space his words sounded like begging.

The man edged toward Pritchard. Then he stopped. "Pritchard," he said. "Pritchard?" and there was something kinder than expected in his voice. Perhaps he was a man who had waited all day to come and save a boy. He reached out his hand.

"Stop looking at me," Pritchard called. "Stop looking now!" For a moment the man looked at his shoes.

The air was so cold it burned. The man took one quick step toward Pritchard.

"Julie," shouted Pritchard. Already he was pulling off his boots, stumbling in the snow. He ran the way people eat who will never get enough. He turned back only once and his face was hoping hard against the cold, the taking away, and trammeled hearts everywhere.

The man in black set down his bag. He didn't chase after Pritchard. People like him didn't chase. He watched the boy go. He let him. Still the world went turn, went turn.

Pritchard vanished into the mouth of the garage.

Julie was having trouble with her double-tied laces. She yanked one, and it snapped in her hands. But Julie was ready. She was believing hard. Soon, she thought, she and Pritchard would never let go. Soon they'd be unstruck. Soon they'd pull the light from the sun, and their hearts would weigh less than nothing.

WELCOME TO YOSEMITE

AFTERWARD, ALLISON DRIVES home. Her back right wheel screeches every time she brakes, sounding like her first-grade class in the opening of the "I Want to Know Why" song. *Why does my heart dream?* the song begins. *Scream,* they shriek, missing the C sharp and changing the words, because even to a six-year-old, *dream* is an embarrassing thing to ask. It causes Big Want. It makes them stomp on their own shadows, lick each other for kicks, and bash their miniature wall clocks on the floor. Anyone would get distracted. Anyone could have done what she did.

Allison listens to the news during the ride home, and the weatherman speaks of the gusting Santa Ana winds and vast quantities of dry brush left from three rainless seasons. The air feels fretful, feverish. "Perfect fire conditions," she hears. Allison pictures a doorful, a handful, a spark in her eye.

She turns the dial to the talk-radio station, and a caller says, "If there's a fire on my property, is it my responsibility despite the circumstances?" She flips the channel.

Entering her apartment, Allison sees the overpriced natural fiber rug (the one that *Home* magazine said would lend serenity to any entryway) at a goofy angle, as if a dog just tore through. She sees her newest yard sale find, a little wooden boat with a tiny blond figurehead at its prow, broken on the floor.

"My lady's broken," Allison yells to her husband, Phil. "Did you break my lady?" She can hear him in the bedroom talking to his father, the appellate judge, on their ailing portable phone, walking, rotating to find one strand of clear reception, frantically fibbing. "She's fallen on her head!" she shouts.

"Got back yesterday from Yosemite," Allison hears. He must have just got on the line. The big lies go up front. "It was astonishing, as usual. No, not just for a day—the entire weekend! Of course we flew, then we rented a big old Suburban. A red one," he concludes. Like a person having a coughing fit, he's got to get them all out.

Allison will not say to him, "But we didn't go out of town; you disappeared for the afternoon, and I went to a yard sale."

She hears, "Allison's doing great, Allison's a real fireball, yeah, she runs behind life head-on," which, though oddly accurate, couldn't have been what he meant to say.

Allison stands, goes to the bedroom door, and holds up the little golden-haired figurehead and the wooden boat to which she was once completely attached. Solemnly, as if she were demonstrating for her first-grade class the act of smashing in reverse, she joins the two pieces. Apart, together. Apart, together. She sets the broken figurehead on their night table, head severed from heart, torso still bound to the boat, directionless and bewildered.

"The lady at the yard sale said it was an antique," she continues, although she knows he's still on the phone. Phil never puts her on the line. Last time she'd pointed this out, saying, "You know, I can lie too!"

Phil, flushed, smiles at her charmingly, purposefully uncomprehending, as if he's behind a sales counter selling her an embarrassing product, feigning ignorance of its use. He's so pink that she thinks he must have just got off what she calls "the contraption," an exercise unit they'd bought secondhand. A machine to strengthen their hearts.

"Of course, of course we went horseback riding," he's saying to his father. He turns his back to Allison, faces the open window.

"Look at me when I talk to you," she says.

Phil turns. "Stop," he mouths.

Mrs. Brock, the school principal, had said to Allison, "You have 14.6 hours of personal time left, for which you will be paid. Perhaps you can take this time to reassess, evaluate, refer to your own information, and that . . ." Mrs. Brock petered out, massive in the oven of her heavy wool blazer, stewing in her clove perfume.

"Phil?" says Allison.

"Just poor reception, Dad," Phil covers the phone with his hand. "What, Allison, what?"

"My wisdom teeth hurt," she says, which is true, but not what she'd meant to say.

———

FOR TODAY, ALLISON has been fired. Mrs. Brock began with the allegation that another teacher had seen Allison drinking a beer in her car at lunch (it was a ginseng soda). Next mentioned was the incident where Allison, in an attempt to hush a child on the playground, told the little girl that the trees were watching her, and that the trees were very mad. Now the girl was terrified to go outdoors and had to be homeschooled. Mrs. Brock then went on to show Allison a signed statement written by her new teaching assistant, Sophie, that read, "Allison seems greatly distracted, in general."

It appeared that Mrs. Brock was wending her way toward something via a digression about structure and how it wasn't for everybody. Finally, breathless and almost exultant, she arrived at her ace in the hole, an unequivocal infraction, The Last Straw: Allison had taught time incorrectly to her first-grade class. "Repeatedly," Mrs. Brock said. Possibly, a pack of children would, for the rest of their lives, rush and slow to no avail.

It was Dinky Panko who got her busted for wrong time-telling. Though he still couldn't tie his shoelaces, he'd owned a watch since he was four and had the time thing down cold. He told his parents that Allison said the hour after midnight was 1:00 PM. It was true, she had.

When Dinky corrected her in front of the class, Allison introduced the concept of "time standing still." She said that sometimes a person can't fall asleep at night, and that person stays up very, very late worrying about things that happened to her, for example, at 1:00 PM that day. For this person, she said, 1:00 AM seems exactly like 1:00 PM. "Just another way of telling time," she explained, that had to do with "feeling it." Then Allison told them to close their eyes and raise their hands when they *felt* that one minute had passed. Next, Allison left the room "for at least twenty minutes," Dinky claimed. That part wasn't true— Allison had only gone to the ladies' room. Still, Dinky's parents told Mrs. Brock of Allison's transgressions, and apparently Allison had been under a kind of surveillance. Sophie, who'd only yesterday brought Allison homemade peanut brittle was, after all, a spy.

"Perhaps you'll need a bit of closure," Mrs. Brock concluded as if offering a special after-dinner drink.

———

PHIL AND ALLISON look at each other. Phil is now in the best reception pose, a stance that involves freezing midlurch between the window and the television antennae. His free hand is held in a karate-chop gesture, like a person who might at any moment clinch the deal, lay down the law. Allison sees that the red "connect" button on the receiver, the one that is perpetually inflamed during conversation, is off. Phil's father, a retired county judge, accustomed to inflicting abeyance, often puts him on hold for over ten minutes. Phil will wait.

Allison takes the receiver from his hand and moves to hang it up. Immediately Phil begins to whistle, a frantic, tuneless sort of antiwhistle that blooms in his mouth when he is in the throws of great distress. It sounds as if deep inside Phil tiny piercings are taking place. Allison hands back the phone. There must be a perfect phrase to say to a person in this sorry state, and Allison has many a time tried to locate it in her heart to utter the words.

When Phil and Allison married two years ago, he had plans to work for one of the studios. Friends said they knew people; someone would get him in the door. Eventually Phil did work a few jobs as a freelance location manager. Sometimes he helps a friend who has a painting business. Phil talks about getting a notary license; he talks about real estate school. Meanwhile the lies to his father grow larger, more fanciful.

Allison used to try to unravel Phil, to create for him a refuge where this might take place. She had hope, and occasionally she still does.

A jag of bright pain skitters through Allison's left jaw like a burst of heat lightning. She sits on their bed, spreads her afghan over her lap, and faces out the window—the same direction that Phil is looking. He stands. She sits.

Allison sees their neighbor, Audrey, hanging laundry with her two-year-old daughter, Georgia. Georgia is sitting on a mound of wet clothes in the middle of the lawn. Audrey has told Allison that Georgia is an "Indigo Child," a new type of child that has only recently come to planet Earth. According to Audrey, Indigo Children are so sensitive they can see air.

As Audrey pins a shirt to the line, she cocks her head. It would seem that she's trying to listen right across the yard, the way a person sits up at night when they think they've heard a shriek or a gunshot. Her dark glossy hair falls to the side, all of a piece, and she parts it back reverentially, as if parting a curtain in a sacristy. Surely, she must see Phil standing at the window. Allison hears Audrey say in a theatrical voice, "We never use the words *can't* or *shouldn't*. Right, Georgia?"

In her last moments with Mrs. Brock, Allison, desperate to sound like a confident educator, declared her firing a "proactive entrapment." She felt her chest blush and put one hand over the spot just above her breasts, which she thought only made her look like a lady taken by the vapors, like an unstable, drifty sort that can't even teach basic skills to children. She suddenly realized that she'd made a terrible mistake going into the teaching business. She should have figured out a way to use her history degree. The single reasonable thought she could push through her mind was that now she'd have time to visit the oral surgeon.

The hot humiliation of the earlier afternoon has, by this point, worked its way down Allison's body, and she can feel it like a low-slung belt of disappointment riding just below her hips. It's almost arousing, in a hapless end-of-the-line kind of way.

"We've thought about Hawaii time and again, just haven't got to it, I suppose."

His Honor must be back on the line, Allison thinks. She looks at the back of Phil's head, perfectly straight now, his well-shaped ear pressed to the receiver. He shaves the dark hair above his collar every single day in case work should appear. He toes the line that way, and doesn't swing his arms when he walks, whistle, or chew with his mouth open. Phil travels through life like a midsize rental car, lacking the quirks and strange cargo of personally owned automobiles. That's how he seems.

When Phil's father visits, he spends most of his time sitting stiffly on their rumpled couch, watching, always watching Phil, as if at any second he might make a final determination of his worth.

"Phil, I got fired today."

Phil turns and looks at Allison. "Dad, I think I smell something burning," he says. "Gotta go." He clicks the phone off and sets it on their bedspread, receiver end up, with all its little holes looking out like so many tiny, peering eyes.

Allison rises and Phil comes to stand behind her, grasping her shoulders in a thoughtful way, as if to prop her up.

"Hold on," he says.

Allison leans her head back against his shoulder, and he strokes her left collarbone. His fingertips press the ridge, and his touch seems to directly connect to her teeth, which throb, the pain in her mouth oddly galvanizing into hard desire and want. He moves his hands down the fronts of her legs and up under her skirt, and for a moment he and Allison are simply placed, sending to each other the smallest glimmering flares of hope and escape. Phil's palms are as warm as if they'd been pressed together for hours, praying. With ferocious concentration, he brings them up Allison's thighs in perfectly straight lines.

"What, no underwear?" he says worriedly. "Is that why you were fired? Have you got a bee in your bonnet?" In anxious states, Phil tends to use the Good Judge's exclamations.

"No, Phil, it wasn't for lack of underwear."

Allison looks at the phone lying stupidly on the bed,

gloating over not being knocked off, as surely it would have been if she and Phil could have just made it there in a fit of passion. Her heart feels like some old clunker amusement ride, lifting and tilting, roughly circling.

What was the thing Larry Stockbridge, the third-grade social studies teacher in the classroom next to hers, the AA guy, was always saying about expectations? Planned disappointments. Larry was reasonable and could even teach different time zones.

"Would you feel better if I put on underpants to talk to you?" says Allison, cradling her jaw in her palm. Her two remaining wisdom teeth have been left in way too long. Now everything's out of whack. She thinks of them as mean teeth that push the nice teeth around.

"Please, Allison, stop, just stop. I'm sorry I thought your termination was in response to lack of underclothing. It was an unfair assumption; please strike it from the record," and he raises his right eyebrow, a thing that is sometimes all it takes to start the going toward wherever it is that their love resides. A place that they often travel toward, but never seem to find.

Phil pulls Allison onto the bed and folds himself around her back. He puts his now-cool palm on her right buttock, ponderously, like a person swearing in.

Allison remembers the first time she saw Phil, leaning against the chain-link fence outside her school, Wentworth Elementary. He looked like he was trying to get back in. Perhaps he was recalling a day of happy fun, such as field trip day, when his teacher commanded the students to line up quickly with hands at their sides. He seemed like the type who would have been first in queue and watched with great relief as slowpokes got scolded, those same baddies who inhaled fresh mimeo paper and fell to the floor in ecstasy. And that would have made Phil very happy, because by simply obeying orders, he was considered good and successful.

But Phil had not been thinking of these things. Scouting a location, he'd been simply noting light, space, the shade of the bricks, and, reasonably, where the Craft Service catering truck might be parked. That's what he'd told her, at any rate.

"Now can you explain what happened?"

Allison sighs, and the Tilt-A-Whirl of her heart slows and lowers, slows and lowers, thwacking to a stop. Where should she begin? Outside, the sky and trees are sorting themselves out, shaking off glimmer and rustle, stilling each other into dark relief.

⁂

THE NEXT MORNING Allison calls the extra-cheap dentist whose advertisement looms from a billboard near their apartment building. A woman who identifies herself as Margo answers the phone. She tells Allison that oral surgery is certainly included in the dentist's repertoire and fortunately, there is an opening that very afternoon. "We had one back out, and the dentist didn't know if someone else would stop by," she says as if people tend to swing by on their way home from the mall. Allison pictures the surgeon polishing his instruments over and over, carefully laying them out like a hostess eternally doomed to set a table for which no guests will arrive. She agrees to a two o'clock appointment.

Allison finds Phil in the kitchen, where he is drinking coffee, mouthing the words to a rap song on the radio. With his hands folded on the kitchen table and eyes on the ceiling, he does this as earnestly as if he were singing the national anthem. Over and over he mouths quietly and with great sincerity, "You a sad sack, you fuckin' wack. I gonna give you a HEART attack!"

Such a tiny rebellion.

Through the kitchen window Allison sees Audrey run out of her apartment in her poncho, a plum-colored alpaca affair, her omnipresent red water bottle gripped in her left hand. She waves at Phil and Allison like a greedy child, grabbing little handfuls of air. Audrey is always running, running to yoga, running to the open-air market, running to some group she attends called the Positive Identifications, always running, always swilling from her big fat water bottle, glug, glug, glug.

But her hair—it is stunning. The Santa Ana breeze grabs it and tousles it out like a million gleaming blue-black ribbons. And Phil's eyes, just for a fraction of a second, cut her way, and maybe he doesn't see a thirtyish lady in a matted poncho, but a woman who, when she was a little girl, was that type on the playground who easily linked arms with others and pulled them to her, screaming, "Run! Run with me!"

"Do you have a job today?" Allison asks. She can see a sheet of figures pushed off to the side of the kitchen table. It looks to be the total of their monthly bills worked and reworked. The figures at the top of the page are neatly written, but the ones toward the bottom are wispier, the columns crooked, and a single amount—eighteen dollars for newspaper delivery—has been erased and rewritten, the numerals grown larger, more threatening.

"I might have a job today. Do you want me to drive you to the dentist's?" he adds. Phil looks up at her in his neat pink shirt and still-damp hair, and even the way he sits, properly, with clasped hands, seems to be a way to escape bringing about offense, should anyone be watching. Allison sees this, and all the effort it takes to tamper with one's own person so regularly and thoroughly in an effort to escape poor judgment. She sees all this, and she could let him drive her.

"It's only two blocks, it's only two teeth," says Allison. "I'll walk."

—⊗⊗⊗—

"I CAN STILL feel everything," Allison tells the oral surgeon, Hal. He's pricked her gums now and shot in Novocain at least six times. At the last minute, the fee of one hundred and ninety-five dollars for the removal of two teeth with local anesthesia seems way out of line. But it's too late; she's letting a possible crackpot remove pieces of her mouth. Pieces she's owned her whole life. Margo, who turns out to be Hal's dental assistant, stands by the chair, red hair neatly plaited. With her head cocked to one side, hands pressed together at the center of her chest, her sense of remove is spectacular. She could be a character in an opera. Hal gently places the thing that looks like a scooped-out rubber avocado half over Allison's nose and gives her another hit of peppermint gas. Margo smiles distantly, and Allison pictures her walking across a stage, night after night, playing the part of a virgin, singing her sweet aria as if she'd never sung it before.

"Where are you from?" asks Hal. Allison tries to answer but her entire mouth is pulled, propped, and wedged open. Her mouth that now utterly exposed is incapable of saying anything. Her mouth that teaches incorrectly and cannot say important things to her very own husband. She thinks that Hal gives Margo a sly look that says, "We know how to work this kind."

"From Rhode Island myself," Hal offers, shining a small light not on her teeth but in her eyes and then slowly in a spraying motion across her cheeks and cheekbones. The heat allows her face to relax upon the bones of her head and hang there, pleasantly. Right where it should be. Ready for oral surgery. Margo takes a dainty step forward and suddenly snatches up two small silver instruments. Then Hal starts pulling on one tooth with a big clamp, and in his eyes, which are only a foot from Allison's face, Allison thinks she sees great loneliness, fierceness, and a man who takes pride in his work. She notices the power in his shoulders and an irregularity in his hairline where a chunk of hair is missing.

Hal pants with exertion. "A great steak house in Woonsocket, right outside Providence. Used to go there for big steaks. And big happy hour drinks. My buddy and I."

Something is being passed to Margo, something wrapped in gauze. The object seems too big to be just a tooth. Perhaps a whole piece of mouth came out by accident. Maybe they'll try to sneak it back in again later, thinks Allison. She tries to remember the entire thought, remembers to remember it. She'll check, she'll check before she goes to make sure her whole mouth is there. Perspiration begins to show on Hal's blank hair space, the place where the battles of his life are recorded. Allison feels the peppermint gas beneficently press into the corners of her insides, inflating her heart. She realizes that Hal's kindness is vast, vast. No wonder his assistant sings for free each night.

Hal throws his entire weight into pulling out the next tooth. It seems that Allison's head may come free of her body, her body flung across the room, the chair ripped out of the floor. Margo hands him what looks like a small ice pick. Alarmless, she smiles in a professionally sweet way and absently pats the arm of the dental chair. Allison thinks of a picture she once saw. The image was of a servant in an ancient Japanese erotic picture, one whose job it was to shake the marriage bed for added pleasure.

Hal stands, suction hose in hand. He has the look of someone listening to instructions on an invisible headset. Allison knows that he's now receiving her thoughts. Sure, Hal gets it, she thinks. And Margo, too. They both truly, truly get it. They are people who would understand anything, anything at all, and who with great equanimity could assess a person's actions. They are heroes, these gentle dental folk, who would not think a person was bad just because she left her teeth in too long. Or mixed up earlier from later. Or was a person who, head and heart chopped apart, could offer neither comfort nor wisdom.

⁂

THE EARTH IS in love with the air, for all over town small fires burn. Allison makes her way down the sidewalk, such a short way to her own home, and she's almost floating, for she's free of the mean teeth, and wisdom is pending, and so many things make better sense than they did, for example, just yesterday. She is still slowly breathing in peppermint. (And smoke.) Breathing out peppermint. (And smoke.) Miraculously, the entire procedure took less than an hour, less than half the time Margo quoted her on the phone. *See how things just fall into place,* she thinks. Only somewhere very far away does she recollect the possibility of pain, the type that can fasten a person to a particular moment forever.

Allison is only half a block from her home when she notes activity around the doorway of their apartment. There is a figure, a woman who comes out of the door, steps over the threshold. For a moment Allison believes that Wentworth Elementary has reconsidered, has sent an emissary to bring her back. Maybe Phil is putting in a good word, recalling Allison's strong points, her fireball aspect and such.

And there he is, Phil, leaning (a thing he never does) against their apartment door, slouching even, and his left hand is holding the back of Audrey's neck, for she is the visitor and perhaps needs steadying after her social call. The way Phil grasps her is rough and playful, like someone about to lift up a baby animal, the type that is as tough as it is beautiful. Perhaps he has given her a spin on the "contraption." But wait! What? No water bottle?! And even from this distance Allison can see a particular shiny softness around him, as if he'd been gently heated around the edges. Yes, it's Phil, the genuine article.

Allison doesn't stop. She doesn't turn back. Instead, she keeps on walking. She is walking. *If there's a fire on my property, is it my responsibility despite the circumstances?*

Phil sees Allison. He immediately straightens up and tries to sort his limbs into some clear stance. Audrey follows his gaze and smiles at Allison, perhaps a tactic learned from the Positive Identifications. Then Phil gives Audrey the universal *Don't worry, she's high on dentist gas* look. Or that's how it seems to Allison.

"Aren't you well?" Audrey calls. No one is pretending she came for a cup of sugar. Allison means to say something incisive and shattering, but her mouth is packed with cotton.

Audrey rakes her long fingers through her hair, and it pools luxuriously about her shoulders. No one is pretending he didn't see that. Then Audrey turns and starts down the little sidewalk toward her apartment. Halfway there, she stops, looks back once at Phil and Allison, then bows her head in a phony spiritual gesture, which seems to say, "Peace, peace on this house." Those festive playground girls never did go in much for apology.

Allison and Phil both look at their doorstep for a while. A fire engine sounds in the distance, and Phil impatiently peers down the street, like a man waiting for a cab he'd called an hour ago.

"Take me somewhere, Phil," Allison finally says, and her words, the first she's spoken since she left Hal and Margo, sound muffled and wrong sized, like words in a dream. She smacks the little white bag full of gauze and Vicodin that Margo gave her against her thigh for emphasis. She'll fix this situation, won't she. Won't she? "Please, let's go."

"Allison, just come in the house, can you do that?" asks Phil. A single sharp whistle escapes his lips. He holds open the door with a straight arm. Already his body is brittling up. And already he has, out of habit and extensive practice, launched into his own best innocuous version of himself.

"We'll go away soon," he says quietly.

Allison stands in their entryway of no serenity, half in, half out, and she thinks of a game that her first-graders played called Stay Here! Go Home! The rules were really quite simple: When someone's at *your* desk, *you* call the shots. You can command them to stay by your side until the end of time. Or you can send them packing.

Stay here. Go home. In this case, both the same. Both the same.

"Some beautiful place?" Allison asks, and for an instant she imagines her and Phil as that couple, the one barreling along in their vacation vehicle, so fast, so fast in their happiness that they almost miss the blue marker on the edge of the road, a sign that reads: *Welcome to Yosemite.*

YES, YES, CHERRIES

HENRY'S WIFE IS Sandra Clarkingham. Sandra is the type of person who wins a free trip to France and doesn't even take it: "One can see the Louvre only so many times." Molly learned this the day she signed her lease to the apartment beneath Henry and Sandra's garage, a document that Sandra hand delivered to her and across the top of which she had written, in large, perfectly formed letters, the word *Undertenant*.

Molly tried to keep this in mind last Thursday, when Sandra came down the steps to her kitchen door, the kitchen door only fifteen feet from where Molly stood having sex with Henry.

To be fair, Henry and Molly were trying to stop. They were trying all the time.

On that particular Thursday, they had begun a discussion about their problem and ended up furthering it against the kitchen counter. It pressed back loyally. Molly's teakettle burbled then moaned just before it jumped an octave and started shrieking. "You drink a lot of tea," Henry said from behind her. "Maybe too much."

"Turn it off," Molly said, because he was certainly in closer proximity to it.

Sandra called, "Honey, where's the rake?"

Then they really tried to stop. Trying to stop: falling out a window and watching the ledges pass.

Molly's teakettle wailed relentlessly. Henry kneeled down in front of her and then turned his ear, as if listening to a seashell. Over his head and through her kitchen windowpane, Molly saw a big blameless sky—a deep blue sky scratched white with the thinnest of clouds. Mr. Davenport, her third-grade math teacher, liked to say that the sky starts at your feet—that people think it's way, way off, but really it's right here.

Henry and Molly were way off. They were right here. They were dropping, dropping.

"Because yesterday it was lying across the flagstones ..."

Then Sandra was at the door. Still they were not stopping. Still they were feasting on sky.

"Are you in there? Henry? Henry?"

"I'm helping Molly," Henry called. Molly could picture Sandra impatiently, deliberately drawing the sole of her Italian gardening shoe against Molly's welcome mat, as if to scrape off something undesirable. While a teenager, Sandra trained dogs for the blind, and this foot motion just became habit. She told Molly that the day she first showed her the guest apartment, claiming that Molly would never be able to hear the car pull into the garage overhead.

"Hello, Mo-lay," Sandra called, pronouncing her name as she always did, like the Mexican chocolate sauce. Molly was suddenly struck by the image of Sandra standing outside her door, rendered motionless by her own good manners, waiting, wondering, the sun hot on her hair. "Hello?" Pause. Scrape. Pause. Scrape. Then, finally, "The rake," Sandra said, as if it were the title of an essay she was being forced to read. "Henry?" she offered one last time, but they could tell she had already turned to leave.

Afterward, Molly said to Henry, "When you think of me, what is it you think?"

"What?"

"How do you hold me in your mind?"

Henry peered into the distance as if her image might be there, shrunken to the size of a religious medal. Then he said, "I think of you as *tribe*."

The word graced them, Molly thought, with all sorts of things—a commonality of heart, a recognition that they were beyond ordinary romantic overtures. They had a speed pass to love. Tribe.

—∞∞—

MOLLY TURNS OFF the shower and listens for Henry's car as she does every Tuesday and Thursday night when he arrives home at 7:30 after his day in court. She hears Henry's car pull in and inch forward slowly, very slowly to where a thin rope hangs from a rafter in the garage. Sandra tied it there. It's designed to brush against Henry's windshield at the exact moment when the stopping should take place.

—∞∞—

THE NEXT DAY, as Molly walks up the steps that divide her apartment from Sandra and Henry's house, she sees Sandra through the dining room window, lying on the dining room floor. Just lying. It looks like Sandra is watching her mahogany china cabinet, a piece that features at its top two identical pieces of carved wood that face each other like twin brontosauruses. Between them stands a spindly little wooden column, seemingly the object of their mutual desire.

"Sandra?" Molly calls. Molly sees Sandra's left hand dart out. But she does not turn her head or answer. Perhaps she's fallen or fainted. Or worse. Molly runs around to the front of the house, a house into which she has never been invited.

Set into the upper half of Henry and Sandra's front door is a pane of antique glass that Sandra had shipped directly from a Spanish monastery. She told Molly that the day

Molly dropped off her security deposit. Through it, Molly can still see Sandra, but due to a distortion, Sandra appears like a small figure trapped in a paperweight. Molly opens the door, which is unlocked.

Lying on the floor in her crisp blue cotton slacks and pinstriped shirt, Sandra looks like a toppled mannequin, and suddenly it occurs to Molly that there isn't even a table or chairs in this room. Though there are other pieces of furniture—a sideboard, a server, as well as a tumble of ancient fireplace pokers and some expensive-looking tapestry pillows all come to a stop against the wall. There is no comfort here.

"My mother had such an eye, she could spot an uneven skirt hem from across the room," Sandra says. "I mention this because for the first time I realize how crooked these floorboards actually are." One slender index finger, the color of skim milk, flies to her left eye.

"Sandra, are you all right?" asks Molly. She notices a shoe box on the sideboard behind Sandra labeled String Too Short to Use.

"Who will take care of me?" The pale hand returns to the floor, palm side up. "Who?" Sandra repeats as she looks at Molly and inhales in a disorganized, fitful way. She looks to the side as if she wants to turn her head but can't.

Earlier that month, Henry told Molly that he and Sandra once took a nighttime stroll and a streetlight went out as they approached it. Sandra, he said, had thought that she caused it, so powerful was her personal energy. The *arrogance,* Molly thought, the arrogance. And certainly that made it easier to betray her.

We never take walks anymore, Henry had then assured Molly. We don't even kiss.

Sandra's narrow back looks indefensible, swathed in thin blue stripes like so many tiny hearts flatlining. It seems to Molly that she should cover her, but there is no blanket or throw in sight.

"Sometimes I get these terrible muscle spasms. Sometimes I have to lie on the floor." Sandra stares at a photograph on the wall.

Molly steps closer to see the picture of a young child at the beach, wearing a seaweed skirt. Laughing. Pointing at the camera.

"Is that you, Sandra?"

"No, that's Henry. His father took that picture." And Molly can see that the boy in the picture was loved, at least at that moment. For some reason she'd always thought Henry had had a hard childhood. He once told her how his father had bought him a new television set from some men on the side of the highway. It was to be his Christmas present. When they got home, they discovered that inside the box was an old outboard motor. That was one of the stories.

"Could you put that pillow under my head?"

Molly puts her hands on either side of Sandra's head and

very carefully lifts her up and onto the pillow. Sandra is saying something about how she needs to take the old sofa out of the garage, and how maybe she could just put a new slipcover over it, though everyone knows that slipcovers are about "putting shiny new over old bad business." Then she mentions that her temperature runs one degree cooler than the average adult. That this is also common to antelopes. It occurs to Molly that Sandra is on some sort of medication. Then Sandra mentions their neighbor Sue Dibbetts— how nice Sue Dibbets is, because Sue Dibbets took the time to walk over a piece of Sandra's mail that had ended up in Sue Dibbets's mailbox. So nice of Sue. So nice. Sandra reaches up and grabs Molly's hand. "But of course, she's not as nice as you, Molly. No one is as nice as you."

<hr />

HENRY AND MOLLY go to the Barton Towers hotel. Their place. No one in Los Angeles in their right mind would ever come here. The Barton Towers hotel is on the outskirts of Century City. "Only a twenty-six-minute walk from Avenue of the Americas," the brochure reads. Sometimes tourists come here by accident.

Molly waits outside the lobby while Henry pulls the car around to the self-park. She spots a woman's pink cotton glove flattened stiff with dirt in the driveway. What should she do with it? Throw it away? Turn it in at the front desk? She ends up carefully placing it next to the hotel wall.

While Henry checks in, Molly waits on the staircase. Not that it's very likely they'd bump into anyone they know. Still. The desk clerk says to a man, "Well, technically you're at a distance from Hollywood and all the movie stars, but that doesn't mean you won't experience some of the flavor." Molly watches the man study a brochure that reads: "Los Angeles: One Big Small Town." Against the background is a picture of city lights, but it could be any city at all. She can imagine the travel agency scanning in Las Vegas, Portland, Tuscon. The man doesn't look disappointed. Perhaps today he will find something unexpected, particular, salvific. Molly looks out the hotel window and watches an elevator, its borders lit by small blue lights, sliding up and down the outside of the hotel like a single escaped amusement park car.

Henry had picked her up outside of the market research company where she works as a telephone interviewer or, more precisely, a "prescreener." She'd spent the last week calling and interviewing more than two hundred women for a focus group on wine labels.

The client had wanted very particular women in the group: over forty, thought they knew something about wine but not real connoisseurs, willing to pay between eight and eleven dollars for a bottle of wine. "We're looking for women who are willing to want." There were over twenty label mock-ups for each group to peruse. The client wanted the label that said, *Take me, Want me.* Half the people in the group, when pressed, admitted that they bought "Two Buck Chuck" at Trader Joe's. It had been a long afternoon, and there had been pressure from management. She should have been able to weed out that type. Henry has suggested that she get out of the focus group work altogether. He's suggested that she start her own business. Perhaps she could be an event planner or a consultant of some sort. She's good at details, he tells her. For example, once Henry had mentioned that his favorite fruit was cherries, and Molly met him at the Barton Towers with a basket of them. That sort of thing.

Molly doesn't particularly mind the work, though. And people seem to like being asked questions. Some, due to nerves or possibly the lack of attention in their own lives, will offer the odd intimacy, will mention a violent son or describe breathing problems. Others gild the lily about the part of town they live in or repeatedly mention the fact that their apartment has built-in cabinets.

Molly looks at Henry in profile as he opens up the door to their room—his secret half face. She can suddenly see how he will look as a very old man. They both sit on the edge of the bed. They come here to have sex, although usually they don't. Sex is for kitchens. Instead, the Barton Towers has become the place where they go to live out the next installment of their lives together in a sort of faux domesticity. Sometimes Henry finishes off a bit of work on his laptop. Sometimes he drinks a glass or two of whiskey from a bottle he keeps in his briefcase. Once in a while he watches the Weather Channel. Molly takes a bath, or does leg exercises on the blue carpet. Maybe she'll write in her journal or organize the receipts in her wallet. But who knows, they might have sex. They might have it at any second.

Haltingly, Henry types slimmed-down, chopped-up phrases. Molly reads over his shoulder: *Cnflct re. prchase Grge Frman grll. Grll hit plntff in head. Plntff fell.* Molly picks up the Barton Towers tourist suggestion pamphlet from the nightstand and flips through it. She has done this before, and she will do it again. Every month, a new picture is superimposed on the pamphlet. Usually a picture of the beach. At daybreak. Or filled with bodies. Or then there's the one with the gull that stands in silhouette. Molly is pretty sure the order is beach, beach, bird. Beach, beach, bird. The sky stays the same, though. Sometimes, from inside the pamphlet she'll read out loud about a concert that's being held in a park or a renaissance fair. They should go. Wouldn't that be a riot? Molly will chatter along while Henry works, and sometimes he will smile or lift his eyebrows. Just like people at home.

When he finishes typing, Henry says, "I went to kidnapping training today."

"How to do it?"

"How to get out of it."

"You mean when it happens?"

"Yes," he says, and it occurs to Molly that he looks hopeful.

"First, you need to break the taillight with your fist—this is if someone stuffs you in a car trunk—and then you tell your abductor about the kinds of plants you have in your garden. It's a bonding trick. Lawyers have disappeared. People do, you know."

"Do what?"

"Disappear," he says, and she can see how badly he wants to be captured by someone.

The sound of a person or persons, stomping, starts up in the room next door. But no music. Maybe the sound is more like churning butter. They both ignore it, the way they ignore the iron mark on the sofa.

"Let's order in," says Henry. The Barton Towers' in-house restaurant, the All-American, promises to deliver for free to all paying guests of the hotel. The All-American menu frequently features entrees suited to an upcoming holiday. It is July 1 and today's specials are "inspired by the Revolutionary War era." This translates to cranberry bread and corn—corn cakes, corn on the cob, corn pudding. And pork.

"Oh, good," says Henry. "I'd love some pork. Sandra never lets me eat it."

"Sure. Pork is great. A great meat," says Molly. Molly: not the boss of his food.

The stomping or churning has mutated into a wider sound like someone repeatedly throwing a bag of mail against the wall.

"You're so beautiful, Molly," says Henry. "You get to enjoy it, you know."

Molly doesn't know how to respond to this. She looks at the back of the All-American menu. No further food is listed, but there is some sort of quiz about the Revolutionary War.

The bright red lettering reads: Did you know John Adams of the United States of America defended the British soldiers after the Boston Massacre? Well, he did. Picture this:

British soldiers rushed to the defense of one of their comrades who was being pelted with potatoes. Matters escalated until shots were fired. Eight British soldiers were charged with murder. Surprisingly, future president John Adams took up the defense of the soldiers. All but two were acquitted by a local jury. Those two were found guilty of manslaughter, but were allowed Benefit of Clergy. This means that they were allowed to make penance instead of being executed. To ensure that they could never use Benefit of Clergy again, they were branded on both thumbs.

Next to this, someone has scratched in purple ink—*good idea.*

Molly is an OW. She finds this out on the first affair website that she pulls up. A site for the "other woman."

Sandra is the BW (betrayed wife) and Henry is the MM (married man). Married-Betrayed-Other. On the survey forms at the market research company "other" is how they screen out people. If how a person feels about the cell phone, the pizza pocket, cigarettes, or a game show pilot is "other" they're considered "passion deficient" and unlikely to respond with suitable exuberance in a focus group situation.

Molly gets a phone call from Sandra, who tells her she'd like to take her out for coffee. To thank her. To thank her for being so nice.

ACROSS THE STREET from the coffee shop is a house decorated with hundreds of Christmas lights. Christmas in July. Sandra suggested they drive to this neighborhood, which gets covered every year on all the TV stations, even though in Southern California the real Christmas in December looks exactly like the fake Christmas in July. In the front yard is a wire reindeer whose animated, lighted head lolls from side to side in a dazed way, like it's been grazing on Valium all day. Both Sandra and Molly watch its head go back and forth, back and forth.

Finally Sandra says, "For God's sake, don't these people have anything else to make them happy?"

Molly notices that Sandra's hands are shaking a little.

"Well, don't they?" Sandra's right hand flies to her

chest, almost crossing her heart. She keeps it there, as if she's about to salute the flag.

Molly keeps looking out the window, but she no longer looks at the reindeer. Now she looks at both of their profiles in the window: Sandra, whose delicate profile looks as if it were cut with manicure scissors, and her own profile, stronger, less even.

Sandra catches the elbow of their waitress as she passes the table. "I'd like a blueberry muffin." The waitress asks her if she'd like that in addition to the cinnamon toast she already ordered. Sandra opens the top button of her cashmere cardigan. Buttons it up again. It's clear that she's forgotten she already ordered. "Yes, I'd like both. I'd like the toast and the muffin. And a cheese pastry too. I'd like them all." Molly can smell her perspiration. "If I can't eat all that, you'll take it, Molly." A command. "And, if you don't eat it, you'll give it to your friends." Then it's as if a tiny electric current has surged through her body and Sandra throws her head back, looks at the ceiling. A bloody nose. For a moment she doesn't seem to know what to do. Molly hands her a napkin, but she doesn't take it. Instead Sandra awkwardly holds her hand against her nose, as if someone has punched her, and stares at the ceiling. She doesn't make a move to get up and go to the bathroom. She doesn't apologize or make a joke or chat about the antique lighting fixtures. They are going to suffer through this together. Then Sandra is very still. Too still. Antelopes keep a cool head.

———∞∞∞———

THIS TIME HENRY and Molly do have sex. At one point Henry grabs her hair and yanks it. Hard. "Hey!" Molly says.

"Sorry," says Henry. "I thought you liked that. I mean you liked it before."

"When did I like it?"

"In the kitchen."

"Oh."

Nude, they lie back on the bed and Henry brings them both cherry Popsicles. It is 102 degrees outside, and Molly can distinctly hear the hotel air conditioners, all of them exhaling faithfully, and without cease, cool hotel air back into the body of the Barton Towers. A faint breeze blows across the bottom of their feet. They could be an old married couple on vacation. Except.

Molly launches into a tale about a time she'd briefly lived in a loft in Chinatown with five roommates, and how once, when she was coming home in the dark, she ran into the Chinese New Year parade. A dragon came right at her. Smoke was pouring out its nostrils. Terrifying.

Henry listens carefully. Maybe too carefully. Henry is the type of person who would never live in a loft in Chinatown with five roommates.

For a time both of them are silent. Henry sits with his index finger across his mouth and his thumb under his chin. A professional posture. To Molly, it seems that he's puzzling something out.

"You like questions, so you'll like this. Today a woman stopped me on the street and said I'd have a chance to win ten thousand dollars if I'd simply answer three questions. So, I thought, why not?"

Molly, looks at him, imagines him telling this to a kidnapper, making sure to put the questions in the right order.

"So, the first question was, 'If you could live forever, would you?' and I said, 'Yes.' The second question was, 'Do you fantasize about quitting your job?' and, of course, I said, 'Yes!'"

But this can't be true. Henry loves his work. And what would he do if he lived forever? What would anyone do? Molly realizes that he is recalibrating his answers for her. She imagines them in years to come telling stories, retelling stories, running out of stories.

"And then she asked me—well, now this one you'll know—my favorite fruit, and then I said, 'Well it's not an apple, I bet you've heard that a few times today, and it's not an orange, it's cherries, and . . .'" But Molly has fallen asleep, thinks Henry. Although she hasn't. She's only closed her eyes. She's remembering Sandra that day at the coffee shop. Her hand across her heart. A pledge of allegiance. Tribe. The United States of Henry.

In a little while, Henry too will close his eyes. Molly will get up and quietly put on her clothes. She'll take one Barton Towers brochure, which she'll neatly fold and put in her purse. She will take her time walking out of the hotel, take her time walking down the street. Some small part of Henry will always stay with her, though, or more precisely, the possibility of Henry. The possibility. The far away, not the right here. Tourist, not tribe.

PICTURE HEAD

BEVERLY PUTS WORDS in jail. She hunts and traps them, stuffs them into little black boxes. Crosswords.

"Clayton, is it cirrus or stratus that means rain?" Beverly asks. She doesn't reach for either of her paperback dictionaries on the coffee table. It's that hot.

Clayton turns up the TV. Here comes Kent Salvey's head again. Clayton has seen it thirteen times since this morning. He sits back down on the floor and puts his hand on the cool tile. Beverly took up the rug this morning. Beverly is his father's girlfriend. She's allowed.

"Maybe they don't teach clouds in first grade," Beverly says.

Kent Salvey is the same age as Clayton, though Kent goes to a school that is not Clayton's school. Kent Salvey has gone missing. Maybe kidnapped, the TV says. From Van Nuys, where Clayton lives. Kent stars on *One Fine Family,* Clayton's favorite television show. Who will play his part now?

"Although they should. Never too early to learn about clouds." Beverly has two beauty marks that sit one atop the other to the right side of her mouth just like a two in dice. She draws a line between them with her fingertip while she thinks. Then she reaches across the coffee table and turns the portable fan so it blows across Clayton's back.

The TV shows a close-up of Kent Salvey's face. Clayton practices holding his head very still like Kent Salvey's and looks down and off to the side like he sees something that slightly disgusts him.

"Five across," murmurs Beverly, "a legacy hunter"—this must be a hard one because her voice sounds like it's slowly stepping downstairs. "You little egg," she adds, as if to make up for it. Beverly says this plenty of times a day.

Beverly had a little baby girl when she was seventeen. She will never see this girl again. This is why she is so fun. Pacer, Clayton's father, explained it to him: if a person has a kid they can't ever see, that person tends to be nicer to whatever child *is* around because secretly in that person's mind they will just pretend that the kid in front of them is the one they don't have.

"Legacy hunter," repeats Beverly. "I've got H-E-R-E-D-I with six empties."

She stares at Clayton, searching.

"Diver!" shouts Clayton, not because he thinks this is the answer, but because he guessed this word once before and, miracle of miracles, it was right.

Today is Beverly's birthday. Beverly is twenty-nine, she says. It's her solar return year, and important things in her life that have gone missing will appear once again. Maybe even as soon as today, she says. Clayton knows for a fact that Pacer forgot to get her a birthday gift, but he won't say a word about it. Clayton knows exactly what Beverly wants for a present, and he can describe the slippers in detail— the pink silk rosettes, the gleaming satin panels, the seed pearls no bigger than birdseed. Beverly saw them in the Nordstrom's catalog and ripped out the picture, which is folded in quarters and hidden in her *Big Book of Crosswords.* Beverly and Clayton studied the color choices, and they agreed that the blue ones were a possibility, but Beverly said they'd fade to the color of old bathwater, and who needs that? Really, pink is the way to go.

SO NOW PACER and Clayton have come to steal the fancy bedroom slippers for Beverly. The gift was Clayton's idea. The free gift was Pacer's idea. From two blocks away Pacer reads the banner hanging outside Nordstrom's. "Half-Yearly Sale," he says to Clayton. Clayton thinks of the broken railroad track behind their house. The half-track, everyone calls it. Once he found a braid of human hair on the track. It was gone the next day. Beverly says punks do magic out by the half-track. Punks. Broken heads, missing fingers, scary pockets. Clayton hasn't spotted one yet, but he'll know him when he sees him.

"The air in Nordstrom's has a *fine* ingredient," says Pacer. Clayton can tell that means Nordstrom's needs to be stolen from. Nordstrom's almost always needs to be stolen from. It's not about money. It's a matter of pride. Pacer applied for a job as a security guard and they turned him down. Twice. What were they thinking? Pacer Bing has twelve years of professional security under his belt and military besides. Although he'll never say exactly which branch of the military. Top secret, etc. "Might as well have the sock folders watch the place," Pacer says. When he walks, his big black boots head in slightly different directions, as if in constant disagreement.

It's 103 degrees in Van Nuys, and in the distance Clayton can see cars in the parking lot that seem to jiggle in the heat. "Well, sometimes people need to learn from both sides of the coin, and Mr. Nordstrom might be one of them." Pacer walks just ahead of Clayton. He stops in front of a small yard with a sign that reads: Matthew Smyte, Chiropractor. Then he takes Clayton's hand, and they look at the two koi in Matthew Smyte's miniature pond. People relax here to get rid of their painful bones, and who wouldn't, the fish are so becoming. Beverly has explained it to Clayton. The big one is the soft lavender color of Beverly's bath-oil beads, and the other one looks like their kitchen tile with ink spilled on it. Pacer pulls Clayton's hand to his mouth and kisses the top of his knuckle. Pacer is a good father. Once when he was very tired he made Clayton a sandwich.

"You say to the lady, see, it will probably be a lady, that you want to check the size of the slipper, and then she'll say a number like seven or nine, and you'll say you don't know what the numbers mean and that you want her to try on the slippers for you . . ."

Around the corner of Mathew Smyte's house comes a man with a leaf-blowing machine. He continues down the walkway, where a little cloud of dust blows toward a black Lincoln parked by the sidewalk.

Pacer lifts his index finger in the air, draws a slash, and this is not a good sign. "What the fuck are you doing?" he shouts, as if the car were his own. "Wipe that off. Now." The man turns off his leaf-blowing machine and takes the corner of his T-shirt and rubs a small circle on the side of the car. Clayton can't see any dust on the door, but it doesn't matter. Pacer sees things other people don't see, and it wads up his nerves. Sometimes Pacer doesn't act well because he doesn't feel well, though no one ever says what's wrong with him. But Pacer is a good father. Once he let Clayton ride his bike into Wells Fargo bank. He said it served the security guard right for reading the newspaper. A professional only does that on his own time.

The man takes a rag and begins to wipe again, but Pacer grabs the man around his neck. Now he is laughing. Laughing, laughing, laughing. Because no matter what, Pacer Bing has fraternity. Then Pacer lets the man go, takes Clayton's hand again, and they start off toward Nordstrom's.

They are almost at the store where actors buy pictures of their heads when Pacer's body goes completely rigid, and they both turn to face a lady coming down the sidewalk behind them. And this is another thing about Pacer Bing, he can feel people looking at him from one hundred feet in any direction. Any direction at all.

At first, Clayton thinks it might be Beverly because the woman is wearing a gauzy pink shirt with sleeves like wispy split tongues, and Beverly has a shirt like that. She clutches a box to her chest that is stamped: Picture Head. Clayton knows this not because he can read it, but because Beverly once read it to him. And since that day it has had a secret meaning. And the secret meaning is this: Clayton *is* Picture Head. What Beverly does not know is that when she catches her words for the crossword puzzles and explains them to Clayton—words like *tugboat, sleigh, arachnid,* and *scampi*—Clayton pictures them for exactly *four* seconds, just *once,* and then they're in his head forever. Soon he will be the Boy with the Most Remembered Things in His Head.

Pacer turns to the side just before the woman passes them, and he makes a sweeping motion with his arm as if he means to let her pass, but instead his arm flies down in front of her like the old railroad arm out by the half-track. The woman gasps, and up go her sleeves. The woman's box of photographs flies open and the photographs slip over each other, silky and gleaming, and there are scraps of her name floating down, and there are corners of her hair, each time the same hair, falling neat and unmoving, not like real hair, and there are pale lips full of white delicate teeth, over and over, landing every which way.

"An actress," Pacer says. "Now that's the life." Already he's trying to take attention off the fact that he caused this accident. The woman kneels down. Her breasts come together, and Clayton thinks of the soft velvety crack in their sofa where he sometimes hides nickels. "Beats working on a tanker, let me tell you that. It blows up your love life. Remember that if you remember anything." Pacer is talking in a quick way like he doesn't want his tongue to touch the roof of his mouth.

Clayton picks up two of the shots and neatly stacks them face to face.

"Oh, I'll take that," says the woman, but she only takes one, leaving Clayton to hold the other in his left hand, the hand with warts on his index finger and thumb. He switches hands. She is so pretty.

"*Jamey Keener*, now that's a nice actress name," says Pacer.

As Jamey leans over, skin widens between her belt loops and pink blouse. There is a word tattooed on her back in purple ink. It's not a long word, but he can't sound it out. Beverly has a tattoo of a daisy on her ankle. He decides Beverly's tattoo is better.

"Can you pick up my sides, honey?" Jamey Keener says to Clayton, and he picks up the single sheet of paper that has blown against his leg.

"Those your practice lines?" asks Pacer.

"Line," says Jamey.

Clayton looks at a freckle above her right breast. It's not unlike Beverly's beauty marks.

"Can we hear it?"

"It won't make any sense when you don't know the story."

"Why don't you just try old Pacer and little Clay. Let us be the judge."

Jamey Keener folds her arms across her chest as if she's suddenly mad. Clayton watches her nostrils flare. Then she puts her index and middle fingers to her lips, like someone who forgot her groceries. She looks at Matthew Smyte's fence, squints. She looks down. Looks up. Finally: "I killed him because I hated winter," she says.

"The *captain* is on the *bridge!*" says Pacer, his lips jumping. Pacer usually says this when he's happy about God. Maybe this means he is happy about an actress.

"You're quite good," he adds. Clayton knows that Pacer thinks all actors are a waste of time. Worse than sock folders.

"Are you from England?" says Pacer. He's looking like he'd like to kiss Jamey's mouth. He's just saying words to get there. Does it all the time with Beverly.

"What?" Jamey Keener says. She pulls her Picture Head box closer to her chest, and Clayton has seen the look in her eyes before. Pacer is *overplaying* his hand. To use Pacer's own word. He always says a person needs to be just fifty-one percent sure of a thing. But you don't want to over-play your hand, and Jamey walks away fast.

⸿

CLAYTON AND PACER stand in front of the Nordstrom's first-floor elevators. One has orange cones set across where the door should be. The floor has gone missing and Clayton peeks in at the elevator guts before Pacer yanks him back. A man wearing a matching green shirt and pants steps into the elevator with them. Clayton can tell he's a real elevator man, because he faces the people, not the door.

"How's business?" asks Pacer, as if he were the man's boss. Gone is his slidey-mouth way of talking.

"Lost one this morning," says the elevator man, smiling at Clayton. Clayton listens to people's voices slipping down the insides of the walls.

Pacer snorts. "Beats the hell out of working on a tanker, let me tell you that."

They get out on the second floor and Pacer stops to look at a display of rings while Clayton leans against a glass display case. The case is so warm, and inside there is a scarf folded in a fancy way like ribbon candy. The scarf is a soft orange, and it's woven through with real gold. Clayton is sure of it. He has never seen anything so beautiful. If only he could lie on the display case and just look at it.

There is a piano player next to the shoe department. He lifts his hands when he plays, like the keys sting his fingers. When he finishes, Clayton quietly claps his hands five times as he has been taught in school. More is inappropriate. Pacer tucks his T-shirt into his old khakis and nods to the piano player. He takes Clayton's hand and they walk toward the shoe displays. A salesman starts toward them.

"What I want to know is why shoes are on one floor and slippers on another?" Pacer says loudly. "I mean, feet are feet." The salesman turns from them, as if an invisible hallway had just appeared.

"Sir, is there something I can help you with?" The woman is tall and wears a red belt with a big gold lion's head for a buckle. She carries a silver ring packed with keys, and in the crook of her arm, three clipboards. She does not look at all like Beverly.

"Yes, my son and I are looking for a birthday present for a very special mother." Mother, thinks Clayton. Close enough. She's someone's mother. Could be his. "We are looking for slippers with velvet inlay or satin embroidery, something like that. Price doesn't matter."

Then Clayton sees it. The leg. The leg is connected to a body that is slumped beneath a rounder of white raincoats. The leg is about the length of his own leg. The leg is sunburned and wears a purple lace-up sneaker.

"And little roses have to be on the toes, pink ones. Right, Clayton?"

The foot flops right and left, then right and left again, and, absolutely, this is a sign.

"Right, Clayton, right? It's roses you said." And Clayton knows that he should say a bunch of stuff about the slippers, because this is part of it, saying a whole lot to people and seeing what will hook them, but he can't. Because there, right there, beneath the raincoat rounder in Nordstrom's, he's sure he has spotted Kent Salvey. And of course this is where he would be. Kidnappers love malls, stores, airports, and bus stops. If he's learned anything in first grade, he's learned that.

They are following the lady's lion belt up the escalator and Clayton tries to see more of the body now that they're over people's heads. Not any better, but still there is that leg, and it's simply amazing that everyone isn't staring at it. He thinks he hears crying, but he's not sure.

The lady is talking about how fancy slippers come in fancy bags so ladies can take them to nice hotels. Pacer is nodding, and then they're at the slipper display near the women's underwear, and it doesn't look anywhere near as good as the one in the catalog. For one thing, there aren't any swans lying around on pink satin sheets. But Clayton has an even better view of Kent from here.

The lady begins to open drawers, and this is no good, she needs to leave them alone if they're going to get anything accomplished. Clayton can see this even though he can't do anything about it. Even if all he can think about is Kent, Kent, Kent.

"Well, I think one of her feet is bigger than the other, so I guess we might need to see a couple different sizes. Different makes and models, ha, ha. So we might need to make you go in back to look." Pacer squeezes Clayton's hand and he knows he should say he has to go to the bathroom or something for distraction purposes, but when a child star lies trapped beneath raincoats what can he do?

Pacer starts grinding his teeth, and Clayton has heard him tell Beverly many times that this has to do with casting aside his crutches: crystal meth and eight packs of cinnamon gum per day. It's a small price to pay for clarity, he says.

The lady holds up powder-blue slippers with squashed tulips on the toes. Completely wrong! Beverly's worst nightmare! Clayton means to clear things up, but he can't think what to say. This is not good, not good, and if only the lady would leave so Clayton could tell Pacer about Kent, because everyone knows kidnappers have to be handled with kid gloves.

"Little Clay, what sizes are Beverly's feet? Do we know?"

A wail pierces the store, and, yes, it has to be Kent Salvey, because no one would be crying in a place like this who had not been kidnapped.

The woman tightens her lion's head belt. "But sir, we sell slippers in pairs, always pairs—it's not like you can buy them à la carte, so to speak."

Now Clayton does have to go to the bathroom, and the boy under the raincoat rounder is sobbing and no one is coming for him, and Pacer is squeezing his hand way too hard, and Clayton can see from the way the lady's squinting at Pacer that she may be on to him, and once a person is on to you, all bets are off. This much he knows, if he knows anything from everything Pacer has taught him.

"Clay. Clay. Clayton, don't you want to ask the lady something?"

But what was it? What was he supposed to say?

"Clayton. Clayton!"

What was it? It was about the slippers. Was it about the rosettes? Was it about the seed pearls like birdseed? Blue is bad because blue can turn to bathwater. No, that's not it. Pink is good because, because—he can't remember.

"Clayton, what was it you wanted to ask the lady? Clayton?"

Clayton sees the leg jerk. Kent may have stopped breathing. He may be dying from fear this very moment. He needs to save him. Now. If he brought Kent home, Kent could have his bed, and he could lend him his Dodger pajamas and everything would be okay, and there would probably be a big story about it on *Access Hollywood* and—

"Clayton." Pacer snaps a finger in front of his face. "Clayton!"

"Kent. Kent! You're safe! You're safe!" shouts Clayton at the top of his lungs.

And then it's like Clayton has fallen down, but he's standing up. It's like a door slamming, and he's the door. It's no breathing. It's done before it starts. It's a second cracked in half. Just a crack. The half-crack. It can snap a person into reality, Pacer will say. The right side of his face feels like it fell into a frying pan. But Clayton does nothing. Still, somewhere far below, Kent Salvey can be heard, crying, crying.

⸙

"SUCH A BIG umbrella for such a little boy," says the girl who came out from behind the cosmetics counter as Clayton and Pacer were led outside the store by two security guards and asked to wait on stone benches. She'd grabbed the umbrella from the accessory department and given it to Clayton. Clayton let it drag on the ground a little.

"It's pretty, isn't it? The nice colors?" She's got a point. She turns the handle for him and the green designs jump around on the blue background. It's kind of like watching spring leaves blow around in the air.

"Yes. He did. So hard his head spun around!" The slipper lady puts her right hand on her hip and her left hand on her lion. Now people are looking at Clayton, people are looking at his head. Clayton keeps it very still, and he looks down and off to the side as if he's slightly disgusted. He can feel a little bit of blood run down his neck. Inside his collar. Feels like an ant. Now what will they give Beverly for her birthday? It's so hot, and the colors of the cars in the parking lot have leaked out. They all look a pale reddish gray. Clayton would like to not remember them ever again. But there is no four-second forget.

"Mr. Bing, may I have a moment of your time?" The man wears a suit and on the suit is a special gold pin with words on it. Part of one word is "man." Clayton is sure.

"Why certainly Mr. Human Resources Specialist, and yes, we've met before and no, you didn't hire me, because Nordstrom's seeks to attract and retain only the very finest in the security industry."

"Mr. Pacer, please refrain from . . ."

"Oh, I've got plenty of refrain, mister. When I was in the special service they used to wake me up in the middle of the night and tell me my mother had had a heart attack just to test my abilities in case I ever got caught by subversives. What do you think of that, huh? *Get up, Pacer Bing, get up!* And if you think that was good for my nerves, it wasn't."

"Mr. Pacer, what type of special service were you in?" Clayton hears the man talk to Pacer in the type of voice people use to coax a mad dog out from under a porch.

"Tanker-related, top-secret cargo." Pacer points his index finger in the air, draws a circle. Dots it in the middle.

Clayton sees a boy about his age walk out with his mother. He wears purple lace-up sneakers and cargo shorts that cut into his sunburned legs when he walks. He is crying in a way that anyone could tell he's actually forgotten what he's crying about. He looks at Clayton and cries some more. He is no Kent Salvey. Not even close. Clayton could tell you that if he could tell you anything.

The cosmetics girl squats in front of Clayton, close enough for him to smell her perfume, which is almost as good as Downy fabric softener. She smiles at Clayton. "You're the best quiet person I've ever seen. You know that? You know?" Clayton points his umbrella toward the ground and slowly turns it. Actually the leaves could be fish and the sky could be the ocean. Then he closes his eyes almost all the way, and the blue falls into the green. Now it is all green. Just green. Now the umbrella is like a big swirling emerald.

"You know? You know . . ." the cosmetics girl trails off, as Clayton knows she will, because if you don't answer a grown-up, sometimes they'll just stop talking.

STONES

THE SECRETARIES TREAD past Allison's reception desk nervously, like broken racetrack ponies not used to putting an entire foot down. Allison hears the office manager, Nan, stealer of Coffee-Mate packets, a woman whose daughter portrays Live Barbie at doll shows, holding court at the FedEx machine, her voice soft and insistent like an old radiator.

Allison's new job is at Beckless and Stope, a company that sells gold mine investments. Cable television ads run all day long in the western United States, and callers can dial an 800 number to receive a free consultation right over the phone. It's been rumored that there are no gold mines. Still, clients arrive, often overweight men with worn maps in hand, the type who will drive all night for a little shot at great fortune.

"Consultants" take these potential "investors" into a private room where they are shown a videotape of men in hard hats, alleged Nevada mine workers, wandering around in a dark shaft murmuring about yield and drill samples. The men scrabble around some on the ground, and then one of them opens his palm to reveal, surprise!—a little chunk of gold, upon which the camera zooms in. The door opens. Another gold mine has been sold. It's all about "perceived value," Allison has been told.

Beckless and Stope has put a great deal of effort into their main reception area, where Allison sits and has ample time to study the furnishings. There are five red vinyl armchairs lined up across the back of the room, like so many semis at a truck stop, and the walls are covered in mirrored tiles speckled with gold. A white Liberace-style cabinet full of plastic champagne glasses towers over her desk.

Allison has worked here since the company started up three months ago, the same week she and her husband, Phil, broke up, the same week she began therapy.

Allison remembers Phil telling her a few months before they split that he wanted to be with a woman "like that lady from the myth—you know, the wise woman who sorts the stones." He wanted someone who'd tell him what to do, a sagacious type who was capable of making clear choices. He didn't want someone who, when she thought about life, had stretches of bafflement. He said people like that weren't "True Participators."

Immediately Allison had tried to cultivate the phrase "Look, here's the deal," but it just went against her nature—that kind of exactness, conclusion, force of opinion.

Her therapist, Rae, has given Allison a specific exercise to practice at her reception desk: she is to visualize herself on an ice floe in the middle of the ocean, then picture Rae casting her a lifeline. The exercise is difficult for Allison, who asked Rae in the last session if she should picture her going by on a raft or a cruise ship. "I'm just there!" said Rae. Allison, determined to be a success, tried to play along in the manner of a game show contestant who abandons all personal respect and yodels or does a crazy jig.

Allison can see Nan and the secretaries at the end of the hallway, fluttering around in a twitchy pack. They all drink pots and pots of coffee and never seem to eat anything but crackers. They whisper about Betsy, a new hire, about the fact that she wears an odd brown wool dress, which she often changes out of after she arrives at work, and back into before she leaves at the end of the day. Where does she go? With rueful faces they hope for scandal.

Nan slowly works her way down the hall and stops at Allison's desk. Allison can tell that Nan is calculating Allison's profile deficiencies, staring at her keenly, like a judger of dog snouts. In some ways, Allison could be considered lovely. Her long eyelashes and light brown hair are almost classically beautiful, and occasionally people ask her if she's a dancer. But that doesn't necessarily add up to "sparkle," a virtue Nan extols.

Each weekend, like some wayward Mom-pimp, Nan trails her daughter, Vinny, from Ramada Inn to Holiday Inn to Marriott, soaking up the scotch in hotel bars with sad, curvy counters, waving at her daughter as she passes by with the doll people. Nan has told Allison that her earnings go for small improvements that make her daughter "more Barbie."

"What's doing for lunch?" asks Nan.

"I'm going to the library," answers Allison. She's hoping to pick up a book that's been getting a lot of press, a guide that shows how to become more confident through the repeated practice of certain hand gestures.

"Library. I see," says Nan. Allison watches her estimate the salaciousness quotient of this news. "Well. Enjoy it," she adds, as if Allison has said that she planned to attend a questionable political demonstration, a cause that would surely never catch on.

⁂

NO SOONER DOES Allison arrive at the library and head toward the new-books section near the information desk, than she sees, out of the corner of her eye, none other than Phil. Phil and Audrey. Only last week, Allison had bumped into Phil at the drugstore—their first post-breakup path crossing—and he'd mentioned that Audrey was going to massage therapy school. That way she could work out of her living room and stay home with Georgia.

Frantically, Allison tries to escape down the reference aisle with its automotive journals, blue books, patent guides, and health statistic tomes.

Allison can hear Audrey and Phil calling, "Little Georgia, Little Georgia," as she tries to toddle free from them in the stacks. Apparently, the three are trying to find a book called *Hand-Fed Baby Birds.* They're making a fuss and talking about it quite loudly. People on a bright mission.

Allison hears Audrey ask at the information desk, "Isn't it possible that another branch might have the book, if the computer shows three?" A wise woman, a real extrapolator, it seems.

Allison is almost running, heading back toward the library entrance, wishing she wasn't in heels, wishing she was in something fresh and practical, like the white sweatshirt and spiritual-looking loose pants Audrey's wearing, for example.

The air outside the library is filled with a bright, hot jumpiness. Disorder is possible. Allison steps out on the sidewalk and tries to locate her car. She rushes past a woman in green shoes who is hawking beneficence to the library exiters. There's a program involved, something about child protection.

"It really starts with you," says the woman flatly, as if she were a salesclerk who'd just said, "That dress is *really* you," for the hundredth time that day. Allison gives her a look that she hopes will somehow indicate that while she's not going to stop, not going to pitch in, she's not a person who would ever be mean to children. She thinks she can hear Phil and his new comrades coming with their gaily covered, untroubled bird books.

Suddenly, Georgia runs out the door of the library into the sunlight, chanting about birds, hands, food. She runs right at Allison, then stops to the side of her left calf. Georgia smells of leaves and toast, and she reaches up to hold Allison's hand in a familiar and satisfied way. Her large, beautiful, child head seems to make her almost sway and tip. Momentarily, Allison feels as if she'd do anything for Georgia; she'd take the very best care.

Georgia gazes up into Allison's face and abruptly drops her hand. Then she runs toward the woman in green shoes.

Audrey is in the door of the library, and she's calling Georgia, and she's calling Phil, as if to hail her past and future lives together. The solicitation woman jerks around to see her next potential donor and knocks over her coffee can of donations. Change of all sizes is dumped on the pavement, and Georgia makes a break for the bright pile of little cash.

Then Phil is in the door of the library, standing with his hand on the oversized door handle, as if he owns the place, as if he in fact wrote all the books.

Audrey is going into a scholarly, bizarre explanation to her daughter about money. It involves Susan B. Anthony, energy circulating, birds flying freely, and paying for college. The normalcy, the neighborliness of the entire scene, the way that Allison knows that Phil is judging her harshly as she stands on the outskirts of his happy group, causes Allison to pick up a stone and throw it. In her mind this stone throwing will present her as a carefree, joyful person, a True Participator in library fun.

But suddenly Georgia makes a break and runs to Phil. And just at that moment, Allison's stone is making its way through the air, much lower than the ecstatic-looking upsweep she'd intended. It collides with the child's smooth forehead.

The way Allison sees this particular moment unfold is that Georgia rises up to meet the stone, like she's doing some kind of loopy volleyball return with her big, fat, beautiful third eye, so that the whole thing seems almost silly and wonderful for a minute. But then there is Georgia's quiet, a horrible clear pause in which she looks up at the sky with no hurt at all and only fascination. Before she starts screaming.

———◦◦◦◦———

THE FIRST TIME Allison went to Topanga Canyon to be counseled by Rae, she found her standing outside her office, a one-room cottage annexed to a larger house that lurked amidst dejected-looking pines, hiding children and Rae's home life. Smoke poured from the tiny cottage's chimney that day, and the place was lit up as if to welcome a special relative, one who'd traveled hard and long. Cheery music, possibly an East Indian tune, played from an undisclosed source, and Allison noted the real flagstone walkway that led up to the place. Rae was standing on it, waving as if she were a mistress of friendliness, a hostess in an ice cream parlor.

Phil had been the one to suggest that Allison go to Rae, who was married to Peter, Phil's therapist. Peter charged big bucks (which Phil paid for with a loan from his father, a loan to allegedly attend law school), but Peter told Phil that his wife was willing to see people for thirty dollars an hour since she wasn't fully licensed. On Allison's first visit to Rae, the bargain price was changed to seventy-five dollars for forty-five minutes. Rae seemed alarmed that her husband would try to sell her on the cheap like that, and spoke at length about her extensive youth leadership work and "sensitivity to women's issues" in response to Allison's query about her credentials.

While she talked, Allison tried to listen, but all she could think of was the very last night she had spent with Phil. When Rae said, "I think you should come twice a week," Allison recklessly agreed.

That was the last time she would find a fire lit, hear happy, generous music playing. At her next visit Allison was offered a musty woolen blanket as protection against the cold by a Rae who reeked of clove cigarettes. Rae's twins, stocky pale boys named Carew and Blade, escaped from the main house, whizzed in circles around the cottage. "I'm in session!" Rae bellowed. Then she said, "I'm going to kill those kids."

Still, Allison was determined, and she even liked that she had to drive an hour to and from Rae's cottage, up and down twisting single-lane roads that had recently been slick with the only evidence of Southern California winter, January rain. It even seemed possible to her that the therapy would pay off in a bigger way, what with all the extra credit she'd earned from getting there and back under a great deal of stress.

Tonight, as Allison drives her '92 Ford Taurus through the mist, up Topanga Canyon, the wheels of her car don't seem to agree on a unified direction. Beyond the hairpin turns are steep drop-offs, and sometimes Allison has to wrench the wheel back toward the center of the road at oncoming headlights that stare at her accusingly, and behind which, she is certain, better drivers and livers of life triumphantly navigate.

How could she have thrown that stone right at Georgia? How could she have done such a stupid, stupid thing? She tries to think of something else and can only think of an instance when Phil ridiculed her for not knowing that pesto sauce should never be heated.

Arriving a few minutes early, Allison parks under a stand of pines, which slowly drip water onto her windshield. She stays in her car and waits for Rae's 6:00 PM appointment to depart, a tall woman with a pageboy haircut whom Allison has often seen carrying a metallic shopping bag. Tonight, when she comes out the cottage door, the woman seems aggravated, as if she'd arrived at a department store just as it was closing. She stumbles into a green plastic troll, a yard decoration that is set directly outside the door to Rae's office, and gives it a kick in the head.

Allison waits for a moment before starting down the flagstone path. She knocks on the door twice before Rae opens it and wordlessly seats Allison on her plaid counseling couch and yawns.

In a rush, Allison relates the afternoon's events at the library, and her abridgement makes the story sound like the review of a wacky puppet show. She is hurrying to get to the climax, the moment in the story that confirms there's something inherently wrong with the way she conducts herself in life.

"How could I have thrown a rock at a child?"

"Oh, kids have nine lives," says Rae. "Take it from me." She has little bits of orange yarn woven through the two long braids she wears. For all her Earth Mother demeanor, there's something about the way she squints and cocks her head toward Allison that makes her come off like a crooked health-food store owner.

"But maybe I'm a lot angrier than I thought I was," Allison says. "Although I don't think I want to hurt anyone." She tries to recall the professional term for this problem, but can only come up with "Sneaky Rage."

"What would you say you learned in your relationship with Phil?" asks Rae as she licks the tip of one braid like she's wetting a cigarette paper and rolls it around a chapped index finger.

Allison looks at Rae, and Rae tries again. "What would you say you took away from it?"

Allison pictures herself trundling away a wheelbarrow full of relationship collectibles: wonder, safety, grief.

"Well, he taught me how to drive a stick shift," Allison finally offers, aware that Rae is probably trying to steer her toward sex, the only subject that ever really seems to grab Rae's attention.

Rae excuses herself and goes to a small half bath in the corner. Allison can hear a cupboard open, and the soft clank of china—could she be fixing herself a snack? There are no sounds of water running or a toilet flushing. Allison averts her head and politely stares at the blue braided rug on the floor, full of dog hair and stray sunflower seeds. Maybe Rae is the type who makes her family pee a minimum of five times before they can flush. Worse yet, maybe she actually needs a break from Allison because she finds her, hands down, her most boring client.

When Rae reappears, Allison offers, "Sometimes, in the middle of sex, Phil did this maneuver that we called 'the gondolier.'" Immediately, she is disgusted with herself for pawning off a piece of her personal history, just like that, for a little nugget of approval.

Rae has undone her braids, and her face looks much more relaxed than it did only a few minutes earlier. She has a mug in her hand and takes a swallow. She hums for a moment, takes another sip.

"Oh, life," she says. "Just when you think you've heard it all. Now what on earth does 'the gondolier' entail?"

All at once, Carew and Blade run by the window, shrieking and whacking each other with metal garbage can covers that gleam in the darkness.

"You're giving me brain damage!" shouts the twin with the more nasal voice. There is a horrible thwacking sound of metal on bone, then hysterical screaming followed by the sound of gagging.

The other twin yells, "Shut up, or I'll pack your ass with dynamite!"

Rae reacts not at all, staring off into space, only slightly cocking her head, as if she were listening to a television program in another room.

It suddenly dawns on Allison that Rae hasn't done the best job in the world with her children. And where's that expensive therapist husband, Peter? Did he leave her? In all her appointments, Allison's never seen him.

"Look," Allison says. "I think I've got to go."

———

IT IS 7:50 AM, and Allison, coming off the elevator with coffee in hand, can see Nan and her daughter, Live Barbie, huddled outside Beckless and Stope, reading a sign that has been posted next to the front door, which is crisscrossed with yellow police tape.

Live Barbie whirls around at the sound of Allison's footsteps and proudly declares, "No admittance!" as if she were the winner of a comprehension contest. Even at this hour, Live Barbie is in full makeup and wears a turquoise wool minidress, a little tackier, it crosses Allison's mind, than anything Barbie, the real doll, ever wears.

"I just couldn't believe my eyes!" says Nan to Allison. "I had to call my daughter to come pick me up." Allison realizes that Nan's hair isn't teased yet and that she's lacking her false eyelashes and jewelry: all part of her grooming routine that takes place daily, like clockwork, in her office manager cubicle from 7:30 to 8:00.

Live Barbie shrugs and widens her eyes, then tilts her face toward the ceiling in an ecstatic fashion that would suggest she's inhaling through her cheekbones.

"What a shock," murmurs Nan as Allison leans in to read the document, an official statement from the Federal

Securities and Exchange Commission, the gist of which is that Beckless and Stope is under seizure and examination, and that until further notice, "all entries will be considered unlawful."

"Should we knock?" Allison asks Nan.

"No, that's inappropriate." Nan's tone, even in this final hour, suggests her superior office manager status.

"Not right." Barbie shakes her head.

"But what about our things?" Allison remembers a little inspirational book of quotes that she keeps in her desk drawer, one she'd bought at a metaphysical store, not realizing it was geared toward recovering drug addicts.

"I wish you every success in the future and want to thank you for your reception work here at Beckless and Stope," says Nan, using her standard postfiring condolence line, as if there were still some control to be had.

⌘

RAE STANDS THERE in the doorway of her therapy cottage, shaking her head at Allison. Even the plastic troll at her feet, beard in hand, seems befuddled.

"Perhaps you're not ready for this kind of work," Rae says.

"No," answers Allison. "I don't have a job now, and I can't afford this anymore." She had planned to bolster her leaving with mention of the frantic atmosphere and lack of progress, as far as she could see, in terms of her own life. "I just wanted to tell you in person," is as far as she gets.

"But I have some new ideas for you," says Rae, gaug-ing, it seems to Allison, how far she can push it. "They came to me today." She looks very tired, and her mouth has the grim set of someone who hands out food samples in a grocery store.

Allison wonders for a moment about these new ideas while Rae looks at her, face fallen. She seems none too steady on her feet. Allison knows that Rae is not above manipulation, so before she can evoke any further pity or do something like fake a fainting spell, Allison says, "I'm so very sorry, Rae." It has begun to rain and as Allison turns to leave, she slips on the wet flagstones while running to her car.

Allison has driven only blocks from Rae's house, and already she is feeling lighter, freer, ready for large and complete transformation: she'll get a new and better job, find a boyfriend, be disciplined about being confident, with or without the hand gesture book, and what with all the money she'll save from not being in therapy, she'll be able to buy a new car! Allison picks up speed and rolls down her windows. The rain is refreshing, the gush of cool air, redolent of eucalyptus, is exciting. A new world awaits.

She does not see the car in time. It is simply there, as if it had popped up from a trapdoor in the road. And it moves toward Allison's car like a sick-with-love person running toward his beloved in a slow-motion movie. Allison stabs at the brakes, pulls back on the wheel, and watches the crash come. It's coming and coming, and just like love, she can't in any way make it stop.

Later, when she will try to remember the moment before the crash, she will be unable to. She will only be able to recall a time when, as a child, she'd climbed a tree at night and fallen out of it. How once the dropping started, no other thing could be done. It went on for such a very long while. And when she finally landed, it seemed that an exhausted sky had fallen upon her too, squeezing from her chest every last bit of breath, even the tiniest sigh and whisper.

Tonight, as on that night, there are natural, helpless bystanders: trees, wind, darkness. All of them impassive witnesses, unable to do anything for Allison or the other driver. Everything has to happen.

So when this impetuous crash of cars in love finally arrives, it's a relief.

Allison, not wearing a seat belt, is thrown up against the rearview mirror, and there's something ridiculous about the way the cars are collapsing into each other and making so much noise, as if they are hamming it up for the sake of passionate calamity. Hideously lockjawed, they slide at a diagonal across the road, where they halt in tandem.

Suddenly, Allison is out of her car, flapping her arms and making loud gasping sounds, and the driver of the other vehicle, a Mercedes, is running toward her yelling, "Oh, for Christssakes!" and they look at each other incomprehensibly, for they are both standing, doing fine. They were almost dead. But now they're not.

"Oh, for Christssakes," repeats the man, who, in a monochromatic burgundy shirt and tie, is talking on his cell phone, having lost almost no downtime at all to distress. He hands a matching wine-colored handkerchief to Allison, as her right cheek and lips are cut; already she can feel that side of her face swelling.

"Would you like to use my phone?" the man asks. Allison takes it and thinks of calling Phil, but imagines interrupting a cozy homemade lentil soup dinner with Audrey and Georgia. She pictures Phil standing there, phone in hand, shaking his head, and Audrey and Georgia, soupspoons in hand, shaking their heads too, and how incredibly pathetic the whole thing will look.

And so she calls Rae, the most logical choice, only five minutes away, and when Rae answers she sounds delighted to be involved with a bit of dramatic, immediate human trouble. She says with a lilt in her voice, "I'm on my way. I have experience with this."

Already, Allison can hear the sirens, which echo off the canyon and sound as if they're actually overhead, as if the sky itself is screaming.

When the ambulance arrives, a Russian-looking paramedic with a blond goatee runs up to her and says, "Crash? Wet? Sit?" Allison lowers herself to the curb and tells him that her head hurts. Placing his fingertips on her upper jaw, he commands her to "chew like tough chop." Her bite seems to have slid sideways some, but she hears "not broke," and he dabs at her cuts and lips with an antiseptic cloth. "Lips fine. Membranes," he adds dreamily, like someone admiring exotic fishes.

Allison tries to see herself as a regular human sitting on earth, for that is what she's doing. But her insides no longer seem to meet her outsides. The two feel pulled apart, as if between them there now runs a ditch of panic. Even her shadow seems to her a peculiar size and looks shaky.

A red-haired policeman gets out of his patrol car, clipboard in hand, and eagerly walks over to Allison, more like someone about to offer free movie passes than a cop about to hear a possibly incomprehensible tale of collision. He quietly stands next to her for a moment, and Allison notices his nonjudgmental eyes, like the eyes of an Irish setter. His badge reads "Chalmers." He starts by asking her very reasonable questions, inquiring as to her state of being, her address, and her birth date, and when she can't recall it, he lightly presses her wrist, as if it were a pause button on a tape recorder, but instead of stopping, Allison starts to cry.

"I've cracked up my car, and I tried to leave my therapist, but now I had to ask her to come get me, and I accidentally threw a rock at my ex-husband's daughter, well, possible daughter-to-be, and we broke up not too long ago, and the company I worked for has been busted by the SEC!"

"These things happen," says Chalmers. "And they happen all the time to everyone."

Other policemen have arrived, and they're blocking off the road, except for a narrow passageway through which a steady stream of cars passes. The drivers of these automobiles sit nice and straight in their seats, maneuvering precisely, as if to convey that they themselves would never have gotten mixed up in such a spectacle.

Then Allison spots Rae, who is over on the shoulder and speaking loudly, gesturing operatically, making sure that Allison is all right, it seems. Allison thinks that maybe she is pleading with them to allow her closer, but no, Rae is actually *arguing* with them, by the sound of it. What could it be about? Now she's stopped talking and is staring straight ahead, a furious expression on her face. Then she tentatively lifts her right leg, brings the index finger of her left hand to her nose, and sets the leg down, wobbling. Next she gives the other side a go, and she has everyone's attention: monochromatic man, all the policemen, and Allison, because in terms of entertainment value, a drunk will trump a car-wreck victim any day.

Officer Chalmers asks Allison if this is the woman she called to pick her up. "I just saw her twenty minutes ago," she answers. "She wasn't drinking." But then she recalls Rae wavering in the doorway. And her recent mug of mystery beverage. And how sometimes, during their sessions, Rae had seemed abnormally cranky and turned off the lights, something that Allison assumed had to do with creating a healing atmosphere. Had she actually been hungover?

"Well, regardless, she seems to be intoxicated, and we can't let her back on the road, so perhaps you can ask her for her keys."

"*I'm* supposed to drive her home?" In the distance, Allison can see Rae now "walking the line," not earnestly, the way potential arrestees on *Cops* do, but insouciantly, like a saucy runway model. However, unlike a fashion plate, she's falling to the left, then falling to the right, and a sort of terrible skip-step is involved, as well.

"You're in much better shape, trust me on this," says Officer Chalmers. Right behind him, Allison can see her car being towed away by the San Fernando Valley Public Wrecking Yard truck. The headlights of her poor Taurus are smashed in and up at such a peculiar angle, like eyes rolled back in a head, trying in vain to get a peek at the damage.

"I can follow you while you drive her home," says Officer Chalmers, "and then take you to your residence, if you have no one to pick you up." Allison notes his big, sturdy ears that seem custom-built for hearing every crackpot story life has to offer.

A woman in lavender capri pants and matching fuzzy sweater shows up and throws her arms around the other accident participant, who looks puzzled by the extent of her affection. He unpeels one lavender limb from around his neck as if it were an irksome, mammoth caterpillar, and continues to give his version of events to one of the policemen. Allison can hear, "Yes, she came *right* at me! Completely *crossing* the divider! Driving the wrong way in *my* lane!"

"That's not true," says Allison to Officer Chalmers. "We came at each other at the same time. It was an equal accident." And she thinks of Georgia running toward the big, happy world and a stone that had been flung with only the best of intentions.

"You know how many people have wiped out in this exact same spot?" Chalmers is backlit for a moment by the departing ambulance, and his ears seem to wing out suggestively. Allison imagines holding on to them like handles while she kisses his face.

"This is nothing. I've seen humanity stretched to the breaking point," he says. "Don't take it to heart."

Rae, being led toward Allison by one of the cops, appears to have cast herself in the role of social reformer, shrieking about police corruption, pollution in the Santa Monica Bay, and, less cogently, about people of "trust and mirth," people, apparently such as herself, who "try to do good work and appreciate life, and SO WHAT IF I HAD ONE FUCKING VODKA IN THE PRIVACY OF MY OWN HOME?"

Allison thinks of the shining moment after she left

Rae's. From that fleeting point of view, the past had seemed, at worst, to be only a comical phantasmagoria of wrongheaded impulses, the kind that diminish in reverse increments, one memory at a time, until all that remain are nascent, brilliant choices.

Officer Chalmers hands Allison the clipboard, upon which he's taken her statement, and she sighs as she signs off on her recollection of each second of the accident as it flew by.

A fat-to-bursting moon idles in the night sky, untilted and certain above a little human calamity, and Officer Chalmers gazes at it with his imperturbable dog eyes before looking back to Allison. "Listen," he says, and not unkindly, "people just make mistakes. That's what people do."

THE STRAIGHT AND NARROW

MY DAUGHTER SAYS I eat the SAD. This is what Delia and the other angel eaters call the Standard American Diet. She also calls me a Cult of Indulgence member, eating as I do from pots contaminated by fleshly vibrations. Delia ingests only tiny quantities of raw fruits and vegetables and drinks sprout juice in pensive Alice-in-Wonderland sips. Delia wants light to shine through her body. Delia wants to ascend.

Delia,
You were once so tiny, I washed your clothes in a fishbowl.

This is all I've written to her, though I've been at the library annex since four in the afternoon and it's now almost six. I like to sit in this circular room, a shady hatbox of a getaway, among the other annex-types, people who wander around like they're in an orchard, people who actually stop to look at the tropical bird book display. Through the library window the northern Californian sun fails, leaving behind a sky the exact orange of a child's aspirin.

Last week Dr. Pim declared Delia orthorexic. "And that's from the Greek *orthos,* meaning straight and narrow," he said. He seemed honored to be involved with a cutting-edge eating disorder, a purity disorder, no less.

"It's all about control and transcendence," he continued, making a peculiar flopping fish gesture with his hand. He said that his diagnosis was "unofficial, as there aren't yet standard guidelines"—as if a compulsion were a sweepstakes one could enter. Then he mentioned the fact that sometimes a food purist will eat and eat, but just can't stop losing weight. This can result in a "failure to thrive," he added. His hand went still.

I felt my heart dislodge in my chest, and all I could think of was how earlier that day I'd stopped to look at footprints Delia left in the hall after her shower. Delia has high arches and the outline of her foot is so slight, all edge. Like Delia herself. I looked at her footprints until they evaporated, unsure of the exact moment that I lost sight of them.

DANIEL, THE ANNEX librarian, slides a stack of oversized library books through the electronic checkout in his gentle, contented way. For six months I've had an involvement with Daniel. And that's from the Latin *involutum:* to roll about, wrap up, enfold so as to conceal. All that, though I've never once mentioned my daughter to him.

A young girl in a purple jumper puts her head against Daniel's library desk, as if she were listening for a heartbeat. He doesn't make her stand up straight, stop loving his desk, and wait correctly.

Daniel rubs the back of his neck and looks up at me, and I lift my chin in acknowledgment. Last night after the library closed, after Daniel locked up, we became "involved" in the library side garden. We fell down and hurt a hydrangea. We got dirt in our hair. Inside the library, tiny orange and raspberry colored safety lights shone on the stuffed polar bear, rhinoceros, and fox that are fastened to the blue ceiling in the story-telling area. In the daylight they always look trapped, forever pinned there. But from where we lay, with Popsicle-colored flares slowly revolving around them, they looked as if they'd escaped. They looked to be flying.

Daniel stands up, resting his torso on his broad palms. He has hair that is brown in one light and red in another. His eyes are an unfathomable blue, the blue that is the underside of a wave. He seems like a person who once might have been caught in some sort of human snag: an addiction, an obsession, a shameful secret. A person who works hard to make sure it will never happen again. Whatever internal tear he harbors, it has been stitched tight through a willful acceptance of things. Daniel puts out his "closed" sign and starts to come toward me. Judy Kitsker, the main librarian, passes him on his right, almost crashes into him with her book cart.

"How are things in annex?" she says, not waiting for an answer. Judy Kitsker eschews the use of the word *the* and pretends she's British. Her cart's right back wheel skitters off the wall as she takes the corner. Daniel picks up a finger painting that fluttered off the wall in Judy's backdraft and returns it to a display of children's artwork. Construction paper letters above the pictures read, "Things That Go in the Sky."

Do you remember the first time I showed you the constellation Leo? Right away you picked out the star that was the lion's heart. You feared your father would drive over it with his plane.

I close my notebook as Daniel comes to the side of my carrel. "I'm taking my coffee break in a little while," he says.

"I'd like a cup," I answer.

A coffee break is an involvement opportunity. The

meeting place for this involvement opportunity is a small room at the end of the basement hall that holds a card table, a child's wooden desk, a blue vase filled with marbles, and three coffeepots. This is our love house.

"There seems to be a schism between the way you interface with your daughter, and what you wish to ideally communicate," Dr. Pim had said at our second meeting.

"Yes, we have scads of schisms."

He stopped to jot something down on Delia's chart, in the right-hand column, and I imagined him writing "sarcastic, careless mother."

Then he suggested that I write Delia a letter, a letter to tell her how I feel about her, how I feel about *things,* a letter that wouldn't be about food or diet, but about shared memories, or even memories that are mine alone.

I remembered a time when Delia was three and tried to eat a piece of the phone bill, and to make her stop, I told her it could kill her. Such a large warning for such a tiny infraction. Is that where it started?

Dr. Pim suddenly peered in the corner, as if he spotted someone lurking there. Then he continued on, solemnly urging me to try the exercise, using the words *cumulative, emotional,* and *resonance.* Or maybe they were *cognition, culpable,* and *penance.*

I read upside down the only words in the left-hand column: *father, airline pilot.*

"And Anne," he said, "a little humor could help," and he shook his closed hand over his head, as if shaking an invisible jingle bell.

You were conceived in a furnace room. Your father and I were staying at his parents' house in Maine over Christmas, and we shoveled snow all day to try to keep from having sex. We shoveled hard. And we did pretty well until we went to the furnace room to take off our boots. Your father said that someday we'd tell you a sweet story about this called "Dwelling on the Snowbank," and I am trying to do this now, to include him in things. But really, it was incredibly hot in there. I will always associate the smell of damp wool with your conception.

Delia used to say that her father, Quentin, was stuck in the "up," that he was never coming down. For a time she thought she could communicate with airplanes and dictated messages to me that I would tape to her bedroom window. When we were outside, she would wave at every plane in the sky, thinking Quentin flew them all, continually and without cease.

Of course Quentin always did come down, and come back, but by that time she would have forgotten who he was.

When Delia got older, we often flew with him. We were the pilot's family then. We got extra slippers, extra smiles from extra-attentive stewardesses. We are still the pilot's family, but now we always stay, and still he always goes. Quentin has apartment shares in not only Sydney and Hong Kong but Cleveland as well, just to round things out.

———

LAST WEEK QUENTIN flew in for Delia's fourteenth birthday, bringing her an enormous white chocolate lollipop from Switzerland. He forgets that she's not four. Delia looked at it as if it were a petrified tongue on a stick. She lit into him about sugar, about its disgusting properties, and she assured him that she only eats that which is "luminous." Quentin was silent, unused to her easy harshness. We sat around the dinner table, Delia in the chair with the straightest back, me in the chair with the stretched-out bottom, and Quentin in the chair with the wiggly back leg, the one that usually sits against the dining room wall and is for decorative purposes only. I hadn't yet brought out my surprise, a birthday cake made with umeboshi plums and barley, specially ordered from a restaurant in San Francisco called Raw.

"Sugar is an antiluminescent," said Delia. "Sugar causes the same bodily reaction as crack cocaine." I didn't say anything. It was her birthday. She picked up a single tofu square off her dinner plate and studied it from all angles, as if it were a Rubik's Cube. "When the physical debris falls away, so too does the spiritual and mental," she added.

Quentin nodded twice at her, a habit developed over years of striding through airports, passing potential or prior human air cargo. I could tell he was trying to make sense of it all. He looked at Delia, then me, then his eyes swept behind us and he seemed to be looking through the dining room wall at a point in the distance, one that could only be reached through the most careful navigation. For a moment I could see why passengers would trust him, why I had trusted him.

"Honey, guess what you call someone who eats bees?" and he nodded at Delia again.

"I don't eat bees!" shrieked Delia, pressing her thin hands against the tabletop.

"Apivorous," said Quentin calmly and with all the authority of one who can command two hundred people to look out their windows when he tells them to, at some very important river that may or may not exist.

"Where did you get that from? The stupid *Hemisphere* magazine?" Delia shouted, and she pinched her index and thumb into a tight little ampersand, clotting all her great impossible fury into that one small monkey-paw crunch.

Quentin pressed his index finger into the bridge of his nose. When Delia was young she and Quentin would scour the local free newspaper for "Strange Science" and "News of the Weird" articles, and, in his way, I could tell that Quentin was trying to pick up that long lost thread. Without thinking, and nervous now, he grabbed my hand. Then he quickly returned it to the table, as if he'd grabbed the wrong condiment.

"How *scattered*," Delia added, and Quentin nodded again, oblivious to the fact that he was on the receiving end of the worst junior high insult available today.

"You should probably get on the road, there might be a blackout in Novato tonight," I told him, lying, though there had been warnings earlier in the week.

"Oh, we have our own lights," Quentin answered, looking directly at me. "We have our own." For some time I'd suspected that he too was having an involvement. I imagined that her name would be something like Clara—a name like a flower opening, like a fresh white bandage.

"When's the blackout?" asked Delia, digging a fingernail into her bottom lip. She has always been terrified of the dark since, as a young child, she managed to lock herself in her bedroom closet.

"Don't worry, I'll be here," I told her. This is our single currency—her fear of what can't be seen and my ability to pretend that whatever it is can't hurt her.

I looked at Quentin; he looked at me. I thought of us like two people who were simultaneously backing away from each other until we disappeared over parallel horizons. We both still wore our wedding rings, though mine had been broken for months. The delicate gold filigree, which had softened and stretched over time, simply pulled apart one day. It still encircled my finger, but the separated edges caught on everything. I hadn't taken it off or gotten it fixed.

An hour later, after Delia blew out the candles on her cake, Quentin left for a flight to Australia. I didn't ask him when he'd be back, and he didn't tell me.

Delia telephoned her friend Maude, and I overheard her say, "Want to see my birthday cake?" and I felt for a moment as if I'd at last done something right, though I noticed she didn't use the word *eat*. Maude is a sproutarian. Maude has two metal cones pierced through the skin beneath her lower lip. I've sometimes seen Maude at the library, doing her homework. More than once I've caught her studying me, but then she always looks away. I've wondered what Delia tells her about me.

After Maude arrived, she and Delia sat on either side of her cake, staring at it, as if to intimidate it. I'd recently found a note in Delia's bedroom that read, "viewed one quarter-cup of mung beans for fifty-two minutes before ingesting." I tried to pinpoint the birth of such rigidity. As a toddler, Delia used to eat only the middles of her toast, never the crusts, or what she called "the bones." Was that it? Was that the beginning?

"Delia, I paid good money for this cake, can't you at least cut into it?" I said.

At last, she gingerly cut a rosette made of apple paste from its base, as carefully as if she were trimming a baby's fingernail. She chattered on to Maude about how by the time she's fifteen, even raw foods will be out of the picture. By then she'll be a full-fledged breatharian, subsisting only upon light, breath, and the God force. Then she took the tiny rose and set it upon the stove top, as if she were placing it on a casket cover.

"You know," she said to Maude, "that whole apple thing from the Adam and Eve story is bogus. The red wasn't an APPLE, it was FIRE, and COOKING was the original sin!"

Delia and Maude clattered out of the kitchen in their steel-bottomed clogs, sinister shoes which they mysteriously called their "Zoros." I looked at the tiny cake for which I'd paid sixty-five dollars. It sat there, gelatinous and quivering, its bland, faux icing, the color of human ears, mysteriously darkening by the minute, striating a murky brown.

"I'm at the end of my line with you!" I shouted after her.

"That would be *rope*," I heard Maude whisper to Delia, just loud enough to prove that she, too, was fearless in the face of me, the stopped train car of a lady, derailed and done for.

⸺⸙⸺

DANIEL LOOKS OVER at me, and I know that he is about to leave for his "coffee break."

I go to the women's room, where I look at myself in the mirror for one or two minutes. The bathroom light is thick and flat and makes the gray walls look like pressed lint. I decide that I look pretty good in this light. After leaving the women's room I turn not right, but left, the bad person's route. I start down the staircase, over which hangs a sign that says Lending Library Storage, No Admittance. I estimate, as I always do, that this sign is decades old.

As I walk down the stairs, happiness surges through my feet. I pause at the last step, and the hall, that glorious straight and narrow, appears like an open desert highway. I walk very rapidly, very invisibly, and wonder, as I always do, about that one long heel mark, halfway down the hall, the one that looks like a body had been dragged, a body wearing a single shoe. I stop before the door to the smallest room in the library, the one that no one has ever bothered to lock. I stand in the dark for a number of minutes and worry ferociously, as I always do, that Daniel won't come. Then I silently insult our place of involvement opportunity, calling it a junk room, a jumble box, a coffeepot cemetery.

But then Daniel comes. All is well. Right away we do everything, everything under the sun. We do it quite quickly. Before we leave, Daniel puts his hand down my pants and slides it up and down just once, as if to tuck me into myself, as if to turn off a light. He leaves. I stay. I am a lady standing in the dark.

⁂

THAT NIGHT I lie awake for hours, unable to sleep. I think about how Delia had the prettiest baby hair—I used to call it her milk and honey. She thought that was a real gas. Her long hair is dry and brittle now, even with the supplements she takes. Or says she takes—twice I've found them on the walkway outside our house, where, after keeping them in her mouth just long enough to get by me, she spit them out. She's obsessed that the pills are crammed with chemicals, secret viruses, and once she insisted that Dr. Pim had laced them with lard.

I hear Delia moaning softly in her bedroom, and I rush to her. As I come down the hallway, I see her tossing fitfully. She sleeps with all the lights on, the overhead one as well as her floor and desk lamps. Standing in her doorway, I call to Delia to ask if she had a bad dream. No answer. I get in bed with her and hold her until she stops. I can feel every bone in her back. Immediately, she pulls away from me to the farthest side of her bed, her back narrow and unyielding, a human barricade.

"What can I do?" I ask. Silence.

"Just stay."

Delia sits up in bed and looks out the window at a bright sky knit with stars. I look at the fine line of her cheekbones, the wide set of her eyes. Anyone would say she is a beautiful girl. "Look . . ." says Delia, and she points to the constellation of Leo, tracing first the shape of his head and tail, then pointing to the brightest star, Regulus, the lion's heart.

"Regulus, the regulator of all good things," I say, as I used to when she was a child.

I get her hairbrush and begin to very gently draw it through her hair. "Do you remember when I used to call your hair milk and honey?" I ask. But now I've gone too far. Delia pretends to fall asleep, though I know she is listening. She forgets that I was the first one to ever watch her eyelids close, the first to wish her peace in dreams.

THE NEXT MORNING, Saturday, I get up early and stand at the kitchen window while I wait for my coffee to brew. I look at the garden bed I dug last month with the hopes that Delia and I would seed it. Most of the topsoil has blown into the house on the late spring winds, and now everything in our home smells like hot dirt. But perhaps it isn't too late, perhaps we can still tackle this project. Delia and I have the entire weekend ahead of us.

I am pouring milk in my coffee when I hear Delia clomp down the stairs. She is humming, a thing I haven't heard her do in a very long time. She comes up behind me, and says, "You know, milk is filled with bacteria and putrefaction. Milk will rust you out like the Tin Man." There is a lilt in her voice, and for a moment I imagine that she is doing an imitation of herself, a girl she used to be.

I start to laugh and turn around to find my daughter missing her hair. It is cut so jaggedly, it looks like she's chewed it off.

"Oh, Delia—no."

"What?" She pushes her pale right eyebrow into an igloo shape with her ring finger.

"Why did you cut off your hair?"

"I don't need it." The hair on the right side is at least two inches longer than the hair on her left. "I don't need dead protein hanging off my head."

"Delia, you have got to stop this."

"It's going to fall out anyway." She yanks out a little chunk above her right ear and drops it on the floor. Then she looks me straight in the eye and takes a fistful on the other side.

"Delia, what am I supposed to do with you?"

She clenches her fist, and I watch her skin turn from violet-white to a mottled red.

"You know what to do with your library man."

"What man?"

Delia sticks out her jaw and tilts her head, imitating me. "What man?" Then she looks away, spring-loaded, holding fast to something. "Maude says you fuck him in the basement." She says this to her shoes.

I slap her, missing her cheek and hitting her mouth. Delia's clenched fist flies to her lips, an unmovable boulder.

"I'm sorry I'm sorry I'm sorry," I say, and I try to touch her, but she turns to the kitchen wall, locks her arms around her ribs.

"Delia, I would never hurt you." The thing a person says when they already have.

Delia cries silently. I watch her back. The kitchen clock ticks. We stand like this for some time, both of us unmoving. Ridiculously, I touch the hem of her shirt, a thing she cannot feel. We stand like this for ten minutes. Then Delia stops shuddering, stops taking in air, it seems. I watch her shoulders, as if they will tell me something, shoulders no longer blanketed in long white-gold hair.

I think of Maude as I'd seen her last week, peering at me from her perch on the library window seat, like a little gargoyle, her thumb delicately balanced between those two metal fangs. She had looked away as soon as I'd noticed her. Maybe she followed me down the stairs, maybe she stood outside the door and listened. How could I have been so careless?

Finally, Delia whispers, "Slut." The word falls weightless and untraceable from her lips. *Slut:* the ultimate impure. Then Delia cries noisily, savagely, as if she's yanking something off and chewing on it, as if she's at last being fed.

⸺∞⸺

THAT AFTERNOON DANIEL and I are in our love house. We could be anywhere in the library, but we aren't. We could be in real houses, but we aren't and never have been. The wooden desk stands nearby, like an awkward party guest. I sit on the floor between Daniel's legs and hold on to his forearms, as if he is a throne. Daniels sits so well. I hold on to him for dear life, a person whom I know nothing about.

"I have a daughter," I say.

"Well, I figured you have people," and I can feel him breathing into the back of my head.

"Do you have children?"

"No. I don't," and he starts to pull up my blouse. I clasp only the slightest edge of his fingertips, as if to pull off a mitten.

"I want to be still. Can we just be still?"

"Sure, we can do that."

Then we are. We're still. I want to ask him if he has anyone, but I don't. Instead I say, "I can't see you anymore."

I wait for Daniel to ask me why, but he doesn't. Taking his right hand, I tentatively put it on the child's desk.

"Touch this," I tell him, and guide his fingertips over some letters carved into the side that read "LS loves JT."

"You would have noticed that," Daniel says.

"Yes, I would," and suddenly I am in the past, we've both agreed upon it, and this will be a thing he can say about me in the future. *She was a lady who came every day to the library. She was a lady who noticed initials in desks.*

We kiss each other one last time, for a long time, and already I am trying to forget my journeys down the long basement hallway, the waiting for him in the dark, the purity of my hope.

—◦∞◦—

As I DRIVE out of the library parking lot, the streetlights go off. Then they flicker back on again. Immediately traffic slows, and I call Delia to tell her there are two candles beneath the kitchen sink, that she should remember there is a flashlight on top of the fridge. Sit by the living room window and watch for me, I'll tell her. But the phone just rings and rings. I get back onto the road, merging into traffic that has come to a stop.

Delia was holed up in her bedroom when I left. I'd stood outside her door and told her I'd be gone an hour—it's been almost three. Another small betrayal.

I pull into my driveway and have to veer around a woman who stands there wearing a paisley housecoat, waving her arms. I've seen her before. She lives in one of the duplexes at the end of the street. "Are you the mother?" she asks me.

"Of Delia, yes." And then it hits me, a smell like an entire dump on fire, like six kinds of barbecue, like cloth burning, like the incinerator at a grade school. I hear a fire engine, and wildly I think that this woman needs my help, that her house is on fire. Of course, she's come to me. I'm the mother.

But then it seems that my own house is on fire. But it's not that either. My behind-the-house is on fire. Though there's nothing back there, except an empty, unseeded garden. My empty unseeded garden is on fire.

"She's trying to burn things up!" shouts the woman, and I rush with her around the side of the house. There are people in my backyard, a number of them, and they're running and shouting things, and I think I might know some of them, though I'm not sure, it's like seeing people from a speeding car's window. There is Person Red Scarf, Person Bare Chest, Person White Pants. All the Persons are yelling. Person White Pants has the garden hose, which has been broken forever and shoots only the finest of sprays, useful only for washing a baby's hair.

And there is Delia, standing in back of the empty garden, up on our kitchen table, which she must have dragged from our home, along with the various and sundry meats: lamb chops, chicken, steaks, hot dogs, and veal, some of which she must have had to defrost in the microwave, and all of which are burning in what looks like a huge pile of trash, but is actually a jumble of grocery bags, cereal boxes, cookie wrappers, newspapers, shredded magazines, bags of sugar, take-out boxes, frozen breads melting in their wrappers, frozen containers of gravy not quite catching in the tiny ocean of milk to which they've toppled.

Then there are the smashed eggs, the slimed eggs, the egg cartons—they're surrounded by a colorful little fence of burning snack-chip bags. And to the right of that are maraschino cherries, cocktail olives, miniature marzipan fruits, applesauce (really bad applesauce, according to Delia, allegedly laced with fake apples and listeria), and glass jars are popping and cracking, but that's nothing, nothing at all compared to the terrible odor of burning meat.

A stack of grocery bags all at once ignites. They shoot straight up, a flaming pyre, and for a second I can't see Delia's body, just one flushed cheek, and she looks so very tiny. Then I do see her, lifting her face skyward, and for a moment she looks astoundingly happy such as people do when they ascend. *Things that go in the sky: fathers, stars, escaping girls.*

Person Red Scarf stamps out a small flame to Delia's left and a man yells at her, "Get down, Donna!" For the first time Delia seems to notice there are people in her backyard. She suddenly looks bewildered, forlorn. Then she sees me, and I reach toward her, this girl who even surrounded by light looks afraid of the dark.

"Delia," I shout, and something within her hurtles back to earth, a thing she would have held back if she could. And this I know—it is very hard to return.

THE NEXT DOOR GIRL

NABIL TOLD LOUISE he had to go rent a video. Even though it was only 8:30 in the morning. The last time he'd gone to rent one, he returned six hours later, exuberant and incoherent, talking about plans to bicycle to Mexico, import satin, buy a plantation. His thoughts seemed to slip over and under one another, until they finally tangled into one big epiphany that included selling black-market satin ("I have a friend who can begin us!") to pay for a trip to San Miguel de Allende, where all the best expatriates hung out, where the prettiest colors in the world could be found, colors that would inspire the satin, the satin they would make on the plantation, the one they'd buy for one thousand dollers (maybe less!), and there would be a side business renting bicycles because "Who doesn't like a bicycle, who?" he'd asked, breathless.

Then Nabil went to sleep in their bedroom closet, to lie in a soft and indefinite way for such a large man. Louise had leaned over and touched his hair, which was beautiful and unusual, locks that she associated with his foreignness, as if she could see his ancestors from generations back toiling in their fields, toiling so hard they fell asleep in the crops at night and ended up growing hair that was as strong and wild as any root.

Nabil, at forty, was nineteen years older than Louise, and allegedly facilitated the sale of classic cars to Mexico City. He'd also been trying to quit drugs for the better part of two decades. Although when Louise first met him she'd missed that, been delighted by someone who seemed to feel so largely, noticed people on the street, noticed their happiness and sometimes even hugged them. In Bakersfield, California, where Louise came from, exuberance had not been a thing to aspire to.

And Nabil's visions didn't seem unfamiliar to Louise. Her family had been part of a local religious sect, the Silent Silo, which encouraged its members to receive "leadings," personal communiqués direct from God. When she was a child, it hadn't been unusual to one day hear her Aunt Desore, who raised Louise with her father, proclaim that eyeglasses should be thrown in the trash (which everyone in the sect did, though some were legally blind), that the family photo album should be burned (though it contained the only photographs of Louise's mother ever taken), and that the entire group should take a spontaneous pilgrimage to Waukeegan, Wisconsin, for further instruction—which they did, and spent the better part of four days milling around a Burger King parking lot, hoping for a sign, until the famished younger children, including Louise, tried to eat dandelions.

But Louise had left all that.

Louise and Nabil moved into a castlelike apartment in Hollywood, complete with turrets and spires. Built in the 1930s, there was a sign in front that read, "Old World Charm," and below that a phrase that might have at one time been, "Continental Elegance"—the "ent" was worn away and some landlord had scrawled in Magic Marker a single, fat *u*. Continual elegance, all part of the package. Most mailboxes did not close or lock properly, except for one from which a brand-new padlock dangled.

In the laundry room was "the giving table"—a card table set up in the corner of the room where tenants contributed items that others might want. There was always just a bunch of stuff that would depress a person to drop off *or* take, items like beat-up lidless Tupperware, tape #4 only of some motivational training called "Sunshine Query," and extra-weird sex magazines with titles like *Tender Chickens.*

Louise insisted that she and Nabil put their bed in the living room, facing the door, so that it would look to visitors (even though they'd never had any) like a fancy hotel room. Their second room became her work area, where Louise sewed white swag curtains, a white bedspread, and small white pillows made from lace and linen remainders that she got for almost nothing in the nearby garment district.

Nabil and Louise, to see them together, were one of those couples that people puzzle about for a moment, then find uniquely daring—poetic somehow. Louise had pale skin and lips, even pale green eyes. Her lack of color was sensual in a way that brought to mind turn-of-the-century words: *vanquish, release, pardon.* And then there was Nabil in his dark, narrow tallness, his shoulders preternaturally hunched forward, as if he were about to take a dive, perhaps at any moment upon Louise and her ecstatic whiteness.

They might appear like that to someone, romantic figures. And often they did stay in bed all day, watching movies, eating, and sometimes Louise would do little dribs and drabs of different drugs with Nabil, as if sampling from an appetizer menu.

The rent was only four hundred dollars, and the landlord, an old hippie named Tony Dalton who adamantly erred on the side of kindness, had made no issue of a recently bounced check, in fact, couldn't understand why Nabil wanted to write him another one.

That's what Nabil said he said, at any rate, and he told Louise to forget about it when she'd worried, and added that the universe was taking care of them, that it would be a sin to not accept this gift. He mentioned that possibly future months would be overlooked too. After all, their next-door neighbor paid only two hundred dollars a month when he paid at all, and had six people sleeping in his living room who were forever barbecuing chicken in the middle of the night.

So it came as a shock to Louise when she found an eviction notice on their apartment door. Nabil didn't seem surprised. After all, the universe sometimes needed people to move to new locations. The universe was full of ideas. Then he left to rent a video.

For the first week after Nabil left, Louise watched figure skating championships on television. She drank apple juice, but ate nothing. In a room blanched by an oddball April light so bright it seemed to scald her damp skin against her ribs, Louise huddled on sweaty bedcovers, keenly studying Yuki Yatotashi as she executed a perfect double axel of exceptional height, her arms crossed over her torso, binding her heart to herself, as if it might fly from her chest. Louise silently urged her on through her short and long programs, her free skate, through a bungled triple salchow from which she elegantly pulled off a flawless double toe loop. Sometimes the television would lose reception for a moment, and a streak of variant light would flash across the screen as Yuki performed, as if to illuminate and electrocute her all at once. Louise watched it, watched it all. She secretly hoped for a leading, but then hoped against the hope, because after all, wouldn't that be backsliding?

She heard nothing from Nabil, and before falling asleep at night would try to remember some of the happy things he used to notice, but couldn't locate them in her memory, and she found herself like a person trapped beneath ice, the entire world going on about its small, beautiful business, all of it incomprehensible, lost to finding.

By the beginning of the following week, her next-door neighbor as well as his boarders moved out, perhaps another eviction casualty, although Louise couldn't have known, not having left her apartment. A new tenant moved in, one Louise would later learn was named Elena, a Russian hair model who had once lived with a famous basketball player from whom she learned English.

Louise first saw her from her second-floor turret window. Elena wore a Metallica tank top, and was running around the building with her shock of beautiful, thick blond hair caught in a shiny barrette, like some stunning overgrown twelve-year-old, yapping at the mailman, calling him her "homes," showering down upon this man (who never said a word to anyone, not even "Here's your mail") remnants of her life with the almost famous basketball player, starting every tiny tale with "back in the day" or "right from the jump" in her little Russian gangsta girl voice.

Louise could hear her over the figure skating commentators whom she found inexplicably comforting and elegant, the way they talked in hushed monotone voices about Yuki's footwork, using words like *brisk, whimsical, sleek*. Louise found herself wanting to listen to this lovely, carefree ice-talk all day. It was irritating to have it interrupted by the clatter of Dr. Scholl's sandals, apparently the only shoes Elena owned, as they ran up and down the stairs outside her door, spiriting along the Russian hair queen when she checked her mailbox, the one with the padlock, two, three, four times a day. What could she be hoping to receive?

One day, about two weeks following the eviction notice, Louise heard the Dr. Scholl's, after one of their many trips to the mailbox, stop outside her door. She could feel the intent presence of human waiting and interest, the beating of another heart. Then she thought she heard whispering, but there hadn't been another pair of feet.

To whom could Elena be saying, "left his *fe*-male, left his *fe*-male" in this insistent, passionate way, as if it somehow meant the leaving behind of a thing that encompassed both the grand and the practical: the *tree* top, the *feed* bag? But a necessary thing, whatever it was.

Then the Dr. Scholl's walked away, and Louise listened to them pause once again outside the apartment next door as if something were being considered. Louise felt weak and stretched out within herself, and she remembered a time when she was six and had been very sick. She and her father and Aunt Desore had been visiting friends in northern California at the time. There was a lot of snow and plows could be heard around the clock, ominously pressing down the street like tanks, fighting a snow war against which they had no chance. Louise had a bad fever for five days, and although she couldn't even talk, she could hear the plows, and felt a strange dead excitement, for here she was, being burned alive in the midst of so much snow, falling and falling, covering every last worldly imperfection.

There had been figures walking through her bedroom, trying to offer her things, although not any medicine, as that was against the rules, and at one point, she heard her Aunt Desore say to her father, "Put her in the tub. Let's sink her like a stone." And she'd only meant that in reference to a cooling-down, but Louise had thought that people were giving up, that soon she'd have to die, and from the furthest corner of herself, she'd come running back to life.

Outside Louise's apartment building, a helicopter flew dangerously close to the roof, as it cut up the sagging April air, trawling for crooks. Then there was quiet, and again she heard the shuffle of wooden soles outside the apartment next door. All that time they'd been waiting, and still waiting.

Then Louise listened to Elena finally go into her apartment and close the door, close it slowly and extra gently it seemed, as if to say that all was well, all was well, and that people who've never even seen you might somehow love you just a little. And Louise felt herself coming back again, returning in a single simple moment, not unlike that one so many years ago, the one before the fever broke, the snow stopped falling, and the snow tanks drove away.

The next day the landlord, Tony Dalton, stopped her at her mailbox. When Louise and Nabil had moved in, Tony informed them that he was often interviewed for papers like the *Downtown Free Press* and the *Free Crier*. Because of his past political activities he said that he was quoted under the pseudonym Ynot Notlad, his own name spelled backward, and he seemed proud that even decades after minor political activity, one might hope to be tracked down, thought hazardous. Louise could see that it was just this kind of thing that kept him going on a day like today, as he stood in the hallway, a copy of her eviction notice in one hand.

Tony held the document out to her, even though the original was still hanging from her door where it had been taped up with Tony's "Smiley" Scotch tape a week and a half ago, a small detail that she had interpreted as his positive hope for her future relocation. And even now he struck her as mostly embarrassed to be mixed up in this kind of thing. Louise saw that one of his eyes was inflamed with a sty.

"I believe in the rights of an individual," began Tony. "And sometimes those rights extend to a certain amount of confusion, a certain amount of suspension of action in one's life for everything need not tilt and supplicate itself toward the, the . . ." He seemed to, for the first time, really take in Louise's zip-up robe and ankle socks, which she'd been wearing for eight days straight. "Listen, do you have some sort of trade?" A certain aggravation in his voice, the way he helplessly pushed his index finger into his chin suddenly gave him the appearance of an aging prep-school boy. Perhaps he'd never really figured on becoming the landlord of a dumpy apartment building, but as a young man had an enormous amount to turn his back on. Louise couldn't really blame him for bungling his rent collections to the point of having to start all over with new tenants.

"I can sew."

"Good. Think about sewing." Then Tony slipped his hands in his pants pockets in a genteel, put-upon way that once again suggested a young man of privilege. "Because I've let you stay as long as I could, but now you really do have to leave."

<hr />

LOUISE WAS ABOUT to leave for the local dry cleaners to inquire about the Help Wanted sign in the window. It was the only business on her block. She'd noticed an old sewing machine in the back corner, though she had never seen anyone use it. Perhaps she could get a job there. In the end, Tony had given her one more week to get current with the rent.

There was a loud knocking at the door, lacking in both rhythm and happy expectation. Louise opened it to find Aunt Desore, her lips working soundlessly and her gray eyes squinting upward at a point far beyond the apartment ceiling, the roof, the highest palm, and all eternity to where the "Great and Secret Clues" crouched, waiting to spring from the infinite beyond into Aunt Desore's brain. A leading. As if she were about to receive one. Aunt Desore was wearing her "good" green jumper and a white turtleneck, one of many that she washed with bleach but no detergent. Louise thought she heard Elena come to her door, and she instantly felt reinforced. Elena would help her get through this.

Louise followed Desore's gaze to the broken window at the end of the hallway, the one with a hole big enough for the occasional bird to fly through. Then Desore made a great show of peering at the door to apartment #202, covered in racing and pit bull decals, and #203, bearing a painting of a gray cat. Started but not finished. "Guess they forgot the ears," Desore said, as if for a moment she were in on a joke with Louise, as if they both had noted and agreed upon Louise's great and deep personal folly. But that was hardly the case. Louise felt that her life was plump with possibility. Look at all that had happened so far. She had come "this close" to living in Mexico. A mysterious neighbor, one she had yet to speak to, had saved her life.

"They got Donna Willy," said Desore. Years ago, Donna

Willy stole money from Silent Silo, then disappeared. Louise knew that Desore would have thought of this ahead of time, a piece of gossip to reel her in. Desore was talented this way, her secret aims and purposes always hidden beneath the innocuous or practical. She'd single-handedly recruited over half the members of Silent Silo from yard sales.

"I'm not going with you, Desore," said Louise. Periodically, Desore would take the bus from Bakersfield to Los Angeles on the pretense of church business. Her visits were brief, unannounced, and usually included an effort to return Louise to Silent Silo. Entreaties, blessings, and cautionary tales were always featured.

"Donna Willy sure wishes she'd done different." Desore reached in her jumper pocket, pulled out a bobby pin, and swept her bangs to the side. The kind of thing a person does when they plan to cook or paint. Or pray.

"Let us lift our hands, Louise. Please. Just one, and I will leave you to right yourself. Please." Louise brought her hands together at the center of her chest, and instantly she was returned to the old habit of prayer, prayer that delivers a person to a rich dark quiet, away from the scratchy upsets of daily life. But just as quickly she remembered a game called Pebbles and Salt that Desore played with her as a child. It involved holding a handful of rock salt and pebbles, closing one's eyes, and very slowly opening one's fingers just wide enough to let the salt pass through but not the pebbles. An exercise in something. But what was it? It had to do with things that seem the same but aren't. Discernment was hoped for. Frustration was inevitable.

"Most Silent Silence to which we humbly bow our heads . . ." Desore sounded less sure of herself than usual, and Louise could hear in her voice that her mind was elsewhere. Desore paused, frowned, then brought her fingertips to her head, as if inside it a little train had jumped track. Then she began to hum and sway a little. The hum gave way to a low, steady, grinding sound that was not unlike the sound of a distant lawn mower. That went on for a minute or so, then silence again. "Let us ready ourselves for April 19, the day on which all good things will come to an end," Desore finally said, loud enough for anyone in the building to hear her free advice. April 19, a date less than three weeks away. The real reason for her visit.

Two years ago, Louise's father, an elder in Silent Silo, had predicted the end of the world—October 9. But then he'd had to push back the date. It was one of the reasons Louise left in the first place. Though for a moment Louise felt sorry for Desore and her mission. Sorry for the yard sale money Desore had most likely spent on the bus ride, sorry for the homemade olive and margarine sandwich that she ate at the rest stop instead of spending $2.79 on the chicken salad sandwich in the cafeteria that she really wanted, sorry for her getting up at four in the morning and taking two showers to steam out the wrinkles in her jumper, as irons weren't allowed.

"April 19, Louise," said Desore. "You have been warned."

THERE WAS NO interview for the job. A Russian woman named Katrin, who was the boss of the dry cleaners, only asked Louise to write her name and phone number on a piece of paper. "And years sewing," she added. Although it was a bit of an exaggeration, Louise wrote *whole life.*

"You sit here," said Katrin, pointing to a red chair behind an ancient Singer. It took Louise about an hour to figure out that the dry cleaners was a front for something else. Number one, the hours were limited—10:00 AM to 2:00 PM, Monday through Thursday. The same dresses and trousers circled listlessly on an old pulley system. None of them ever seemed to get picked up. A magenta prom dress in particular bothered Louise, the way it caught on the front counter when it swept down in front of her sewing machine, as if the phantom girl wanted to stop and chat.

The main source of foot traffic was Russian men introduced as "the associates," and it was primarily their clothes that Louise repaired or altered. The associates wore leather jackets in odd colors, like yellow and red, and most of them had shaved heads, except for one who always wore a green ski cap. Louise imagined that he hid a terrible scar from a knife fight, or worse. They were not like any boys or men Louise had known growing up. Each time they arrived, they were immediately escorted to the back by Katrin. A few minutes later they would reappear, thank Louise, as if she had helped them in some important way, and leave.

Katrin was not a difficult boss. Most of the time she kept to the back room, where in between visits from the associates she watched Russian cable on a tiny television that she sometimes held on her lap, as if it were a pet. She complimented Louise on her repair of a raincoat lining her very first day, and Louise took that opportunity to ask for an advance of four hundred dollars. Katrin got the money from the back, not the cash register. "You quit, we find you," she said, laughing. Then she became very serious. "Is joke," she added.

The morning of her third day, Louise was watching a sudden rain shake out of the sky, a welcome relief after days of relentless sun, when Elena flew through the door. Louise looked at her, at her blond wide-arched eyebrows, her flushed pink cheeks, the way she stuck her lips out, like a beautiful fish. She placed her at six or seven years older than herself.

"The next door girl," said Elena. She lit a cigarette, took one drag, and stubbed it out on the floor. "So, you are the worker now." Her accent was more noticeable than the time Louise heard her talking to the mailman.

"I am," said Louise, and it suddenly occurred to her that Elena might be related to Katrin or the associates, or both. "It's very organized here," she said.

Elena looked at her, seemed to calculate something, and snorted. "Well, you make the grip. Why not?"

"The grip?" asked Louise.

"The scrill." Elena waited. "The big face," she added, pointing to the hundred-dollar bill framed on the wall over the cash register.

"Right," said Louise. "Do you know Katrin?" she added. "I mean, have you met her?" She hadn't meant to indicate that all Russian people knew each other.

"Katrin is like sister," said Elena. "Like mother," she added, as if to increase her importance. Elena smiled at her and Louise thought of her feet that day outside the apartment door. The waiting.

"I want you to know you helped me," Louise said. No reaction. "Back about a week ago. You helped me." Elena tilted her head and stared. If she had any idea what Louise was talking about, she gave no indication.

"Well, I just wanted to say that if I could ever help you back, I would."

"Of course," said Elena. There was something stern in her manner, businesslike. With no explanation she walked behind the counter and headed to the back room.

That Friday, Katrin took Louise aside and said that Elena needed "some help."

Louise was eager to carry out whatever the task might be. "Of course," she said, using the very same phrase that Elena had used. She liked the way the words felt in her mouth—taciturn, comradely. Katrin handed her a manila envelope. The task was to simply deliver it to Elena that evening.

By the next week, Katrin was giving Louise an envelope, which she referred to as the "deposit," on a daily basis. Louise was careful with the "deposit" and did not pry into the details of the dry cleaning business, which she thought was somehow connected to Elena constantly running up and down the stairs, the mailbox with a padlock on it, and her many phone calls, which Louise could hear bits and pieces of through the wall. Elena was a very busy person who had lots of appointments.

Desore used to say that Donna Willy had "larceny in her heart." It crossed Louise's mind that she herself might have larceny in her heart. Obviously, the "deposit" didn't come from dry cleaning profits. She never saw the associates pay for anything. But the money wasn't from stealing either, it was from some kind of business, and business was a good thing. Business was about seizing opportunity!

Louise realized that she had never seized anything. In fact, she had never really allowed herself to want anything. It was a horrible useless feeling, like wearing a cast over an arm that's not even broken. Silent Silo had taught her all the wrong things, she thought—people who spend their entire lives scared of their own volition, hoping always to be led to something.

But Louise wasn't like that anymore.

⸻

LOUISE WAS TWENTY feet higher than Elena on the white metal ladder that clung to the huge cement tank like a long bony arm. The last time she climbed it had been with Nabil. The Cemex plant at La Brea and Romaine seemed exotic and out of place, sitting as it did on the same block as a 99 Cents store, a bar, and a Pep Boys. It was a Sunday night. There wasn't any security, since everything was too heavy to steal.

"Wait. Hold. I am hot," Elena shouted from beneath her, though the air was cool. Elena stood rigidly on the ladder, too proud to admit that she was scared, thought Louise. She waited while Elena stood motionless for a few more minutes and then slowly picked her way up to the sixty-five-foot mark, where Louise stood on a platform the size of an elevator floor.

They'd walked all the way from La Brea and Sunset, stopping to take little swigs of vodka from a bottle that Elena had produced from her backpack. Elena said the bottle was sent to her from her uncle, who was a viscount in Russia. Louise said she thought Russia had presidents. "The viscount is like the boss of the earl," Elena had said dismissively.

When Elena at last reached the platform, one cautious step at a time, she flopped down and dramatically waved her hand in front of her face. Then she pulled two small red glasses wrapped in paper towels from the bottom of her backpack. She filled both to the brim with vodka. "To us! The Purveyors of Fortune!" she said.

Louise recognized the title of a thriller that sat on a coffee table in Elena's apartment. *The Purveyors of Fortune* had been on the "giving table" for the prior two weeks. Louise couldn't really imagine Elena sitting still long enough to read an entire book. Elena was always fidgeting even when she tried to stand still, pulling her hair in and out of numerous configurations—ponytails, twists, and chignons. Hair accessories were scattered throughout her apartment and by her bedside stand stood a gold trophy that was inscribed "Elena Ovslavskaya, Luster Hair Model Competition, Century City Mall, December 2005."

They toasted, then looked out over the city as evening approached, as the air seemed not to darken as much as thicken, as billboards of purses, sneakers, and a male model lying in the sand—astonished, as if he'd been flung out of the sky—were swallowed up by the night.

Elena told Louise she was getting out of the hair world now that business was so good. "But," she said, sighing, "could all end tomorrow." She stretched her legs out on the platform. Elena had a habit of making such statements. It lent her a weary sophistication.

"To the end. To the end of the world." Louise lifted her glass. She told Elena how she had been taught as a child that when the world came to an end, birds would fly upside down. That's what would happen and that's how you would know.

"Then what?" asked Elena.

"Then you die." It seemed incredibly funny to them both, and they drank some more vodka.

They were on their third refill when Elena said, "My parents tried to sell me once. For the grip." They heard a police car blare, its siren on triple-time, sounding like a video game gun. Elena started in on a long and complicated story. There were many twists and turns—money for fake passports was involved, an escape, living in a bakery basement, being forced to sell cracker bread. She said she'd never been to school past eighth grade. She'd only really learned proper English from the famous basketball player. Her story sounded oddly familiar to Louise, although she had no idea why.

"I'm sorry for you," said Louise. "I'm sorry for your life." Elena sat staring straight ahead, her hand over her mouth. They were quiet for a long time. The idea that they were not in any shape to climb back down the ladder was a foregone conclusion.

"But look at you now," Louise added, and she meant this in the best way.

"You," said Elena, suddenly heartened. "You are like me. The survivor! And the survivor takes always for herself." The rest of what Elena said made less sense, but it had to do with Louise becoming her business partner, and buying a condo in Malibu that she planned to purchase with money she was saving very fast. "You can live there, too!" she said to Louise just before she fell asleep.

The only other job Louise had had before now was as a waitress. It was hard work and she'd never been able to save very much. Certainly not fast enough to buy a condo in Malibu. Louise thought about living on the beach. She pictured white silk curtains blowing in the wind. And aqua accents. Aqua accents were always featured in beach houses—certainly in any style magazine she'd ever read. She thought of her life going forward, her life as a survivor, a wise survivor staring out across the ocean. Really, anything was possible now.

Elena's chin fell on her chest. Very carefully, Louise tilted it back. She kept guard as the city gathered light from every corner, until there was a brightening of matters, wild and complete, as the silhouettes of buildings sharpened, razorlike, and the billboards burst into color.

⁓

THE DAY BOILED to a start. April 19. It was as if summer was already used up, and it was barely spring. The client lived in a metal house with no windows. It was modern and sleek, indifferent to the sun, which fell down upon it. Louise made a mental note to remember not to touch it.

This was a promotion in a way—a simple drop-off, but Louise was going to carry it out. Elena said that Louise would be good at this line of work because she looked like the "soap lady," the type that people simply trust on sight. She'd already gone with Elena a few times now and watched what she did. There were lots of small things to remember, like making sure the client gave their "nickname" when they phoned in the order. The nickname was their real first name and their street name. Today they were here to see Bob Vista.

A maid in a tangerine-colored uniform opened the metal door, which was so polished Louise could see herself in it. "Hello. Yes, we have an appointment with Mr. Vista," she said. A mistake. The nickname was for phone purposes only.

The maid squinted. "Wrong one," she said, and started to shut the door.

"But Bob, he is here. Just Bob?" asked Elena.

"Yes. A Bob is here," said the maid, and she immediately seemed remorseful for saying so.

"*That* Bob. We're here for *that* Bob," said Louise. She was determined to show Elena that she could carry out a piece of business that in her mind wasn't that much different than delivering a pizza. That's what she'd told herself anyway.

Bob's legs hung over the end of the sofa by a good foot and a half. His fly was open and his long dark head, turned sideways, reminded Louise of a horse. Louise stood over him. "Bob. Delivery," she said.

"Wake him first," said Elena. Louise tried to shake him. It was like trying to shake a park bench.

"Fuck the shit," said Elena.

They scoured the room, opening desk drawers, and they looked in his wallet, which was on the coffee table. Empty. Louise studied his license. The famous basketball player. Elena certainly didn't act like this was someone she had lived with for two years. She scrounged Bob's pockets for the money and told Louise there was no way they'd leave the "stock" when he was such a dumbass as to not leave them the grip. "Point!" she added.

"Period," said Louise. "Period is what you mean." Elena looked at her, undid his wristwatch, and put in her pocket.

———

"IT'S NO ROLLIE," said the man. He was small and chubby, and sat on his cracked red leather stool like a little troll king. He flipped the watch over using one hand. "Scratch," he said. A long sigh. "I don't know, maybe two." His skin looked dusty, and he acted aggravated, as if ten people had already come by today with the very same watch.

"Twenty-five hundred," said Louise, quoting a figure that Elena had given her. Elena passed an index finger over her pursed lips. A sign of approval.

"Twenty-four."

"Twenty-four fifty," said Louise. The man brought down his pudgy fist on the counter like a gavel, and Louise realized that she got her price. She watched carefully as he counted out the money, though she couldn't bring herself to touch it when he finished. It was hard to justify selling Bob's watch as "business." She thought of Donna Willy, her apron pocket stuffed with dollar bills from the Sunday collection basket. It was still the moment *before* "too late"— that immutable axis upon which guilt, grief, and recklessness spin. Some of the bills were rumpled and stained. *Dirty money,* Desore would say. Although, she would say that about any money.

"Payday!" said Elena, pressing her knuckle into Louise's back. Louise grabbed the bills in one hand. Then it was the moment *after.* And immediately the word *Sin!* popped into her head, not unlike the words *Bingo!* or *Eureka!*

THEY EACH ORDERED the most expensive thing on the menu. Steak for Elena, lobster for Louise. It would barely make a dent in the money they got from pawning Bob's wristwatch. The restaurant, set on a side street in Beverly Hills, was called Slink, and Elena said she'd been here many times, and was "in good" with someone named Salvatore. Maybe Salvatore could comp them. Not that they couldn't pay, but why not. So on and on they ordered, a bottle of Perriet Jouet, two orders of cilantro shrimp, shiitake mushrooms with cabernet sauce, an order of white asparagus almondine, crab cakes, mashed potatoes. Elena said that they should order anything that caught their interest, even if they only took a single bite.

"You can get Salvatore for me?" Elena asked their waitress, who had identified herself as Paige. Paige walked in a dreamy way, as if she awoke from a nap. She'd been slow to take their order, and Elena twice snapped her fingers at her.

"I'm sorry, I don't know who that is," said Paige.

"Salvatore," Elena said, including Louise in her look. "He is boss."

"I don't think so." Paige briefly touched her ear, as if she were wearing a wire, as if the person on the other end would get a real kick out of these two.

"Please check. You will see. Now." Elena's voice was rising, and two older women at the next table turned to look. One wore a gray sheath dress and pearls and one wore a tailored black suit and pearls. They'd been speaking in hushed tones, as if in attendance at some sort of ceremony that required great respect and concentration. The one in the gray dress rolled her eyes. Louise had earlier seen her mimic the dramatic way Elena used her hands in conversation. Wordlessly, Paige turned and headed to the kitchen.

"Some men came to your door this morning," Louise told Elena. She didn't mention that one of them was an "associate," as only Katrin had ever used that word. She also

didn't mention that they took turns cursing and knocking
for more than five minutes. One of the men had kicked
Elena's door before he left. Louise cracked her own door
as she heard them walk downstairs. All she caught was a
glimpse of a green ski cap. Louise was pretty sure Elena had
been there the whole time. She'd heard her Dr. Scholl's
clomping around just moments before their arrival.

"I know," said Elena. "Sometimes I am not in." She
lifted her chin. Louise considered whether she should
push the issue. People often came in the middle of the
night to Elena's door and occasionally there were strange
noises—people who were chattering a mile a minute, or
laughing, or drunk, or all of the above. But no one had ever
sounded so angry.

Paige appeared. "Salvatore can't come out right now,"
she said. "He's busy washing dishes." A smirk.

Elena shrugged. "Of course," she said, as if this had all
been an elaborate joke on Paige. But after Paige left, she
sunk into her seat and glared at the women at the next
table, unmoving, not even blinking. The two had been
dawdling over coffee, but this was enough to make them
leave. Elena snorted with satisfaction. Louise paid their bill,
$278.35, with the cash from the pawn shop. She took the
change and the rest of the money from pawning Bob's
watch and carefully turned all the Franklins in the same
direction. Nabil had once told her that it brought a person good luck.

Elena stood up and headed toward the door of the restaurant. Louise saw her quickly lean into the table where the two women had sat, and for a moment Louise thought she was going to sit back down again. Elena would find it funny to do something like that, to start all over again with Paige. But Elena wasn't sitting down. She was taking Paige's tip. She did this as quickly and simply as if she were taking a mint. Then she turned once and looked at Louise, and there was something like pride in her look, something that said *I'll get mine.*

Louise watched Elena push her way past a busboy and she thought of the little Russian girl selling bags of cracker bread. She could see it so clearly, almost as if she had been there. Then it came to her. She *had* seen it. In a TV movie. One day when the ice skating coverage was delayed she had seen it on Hallmark Hall of Fame. Elena had ripped off her own life story.

"YOU SHOULDN'T HAVE taken that money. Not from a waitress," said Louise.

Elena looked at her, puzzled. "Well. Sorry to break your day," she said. They had taken a taxi all the way from Beverly Hills and were standing at the corner of their street. Neither one had said much on the trip back. The street was empty. Then a long maroon car with tinted windows flashed past them. Louise felt a sudden sharp rush inside herself, as if her blood were running backward. Then it was gone. It would remind her of a leading, if she still believed in that sort of thing.

Louise looked at Elena. What kind of woman would she be in five years? Louise pictured her as the boss of the dry cleaners, but fatter, hair brittle and bleached, just the collection lady then.

They walked in silence the half block to their building. Elena held her phone up to her ear and checked her messages, nodding her head as she listened. Then she snapped her phone shut and jammed it in her back pocket. She turned to Louise. "Look," she said. "I would not take from *you*. I would not take the food from *your* mouth," she said, her voice cracking. And that much was probably true, if the only thing that was.

The maroon car rumbled up behind them. Then it was beside them. The driver's side window went down. Two men. Two men in profile. One green ski cap. Elena waved. Green ski cap looked at Elena like a dog that's about to attack. Elena walked faster. The car swerved across the street, blocking the driveway to their apartment building.

Elena lifted both hands. "Hey!" she said. "Hey!" She walked straight toward the car. Just her style.

Louise stopped. She stopped so much she might as well have been hit by a truck. Then she turned and walked in the opposite direction. As if she'd never known Elena. As if she'd never even met her. She walked as if she might be shot in the back. She walked as if the street might ignite. She walked like the most normal person in America who never did anything and didn't know anyone. She clutched her purse to her chest, as if that somehow made her legs go. And with every step she left Elena behind. Elena shouting in Russian. Elena shouting in English. Elena laughing. Of course, she would be laughing.

TRIAGE

THE PLANE BANKS, and for a moment the passengers are awash in a soft melon-colored light, one that glides over every single person, impartial and generous. Each flyer gets an equal share, and they are all on tilt. All are afforded the same crooked view, the only one available.

Allison is handed her coffee by the flight attendant whose name tag reads Lottie Childs. A sudden air pocket, the banking, none of it throws Lottie. She stands her ground like a little saint glued to the dashboard.

"Is the coffee the right color?" Lottie asks. Allison pictures Lottie as she might have been in grade school, with the same bangs and two stiff golden curls hanging like savage fishhooks on either side of her face. She can see Lottie gripping her Crayola, tongue pinned between her front teeth, coloring correctly, staying right inside the outline of a big fluffy bunny.

"Actually, could I have another splash of milk?" says Allison. The tiniest of scowls skitters around the right-hand corner of Lottie's orange lips.

"Absolutely not!" teases Lottie. She pours Allison one single drop, asking, "Is that it?" Then adding just one more she says, "Is that it?" Allison pictures Lottie back at her school desk coloring Mr. Rabbit, pressing down so hard with her crayon that she tears Mr. Rabbit's ears in half.

As Lottie rolls away with her cart, the plane gains altitude, and Allison sees Nahant as they fly over it. The land and scattered ponds look like the fabric of a huge, tired family couch, one that originally a snappy plaid, is now faded unevenly with its stripes drifting apart, then randomly appearing again, the entire piece of cloth stained by odd shapes, as if someone had lain down on the couch and just cried for a while.

Earlier that day, Allison had missed her plane. She was supposed to have departed Boston at 8:00 AM and arrived at 11:00 AM in Los Angeles. But she somehow misread the ticket and arrived at Logan Airport with her mother, Camille, and Aunt Tuley in time for an 11:00 AM departure. Tuley, learning of the mix-up, offered no ideas and said she was going to go get a drink while Allison and her mother sorted things out. Tuley has lived with Allison's mother for well over a decade now. Some years ago she moved into Allison's old bedroom and started wearing Allison's clothes, including a pair of chartreuse bell-bottoms, which she was, in fact, wearing today.

After half an hour at the ticket counter, Allison was told that yes, they could accommodate her and put her on the next flight out. And no, she wouldn't be charged extra. The next flight would be in three hours, just short enough time to not return home, just long enough time to sap the life out of a merry and swift goodbye. "You might enjoy lunch at one of our new eateries," said the man, pointing toward a large archway, beyond which lay a number of restaurants and fancy new stores. But they'd just eaten breakfast; this was supposed to be the seeing-off portion of the day. Allison's mother pressed her index finger to her right cheekbone, the kind of distress signal one lady-in-waiting might send to another.

"Oh, that doesn't suit," she said.

Right then, Allison told her that she was sure she'd get a standby flight, maybe even the very next one. She told her to go on. She'd be fine.

"I'll wait with you," said her mother. "And when Tuley returns, she will wait, too."

To Allison it seems that for every day she visits home, a year of mental capacity is taken from her life, in terms of the way her mother treats her. Just that morning in the kitchen, her mother had shrieked at her as she'd walked toward the stove, "What are you doing over there?"

"I'm going to make tea," Allison replied. "Can't I do that? Can't I make tea?"

"Oh, it's best that you wait for Tuley to make more coffee," her mother said. "Anyway, tea is a nervous person's drink."

At that, Tuley had shuffled through, implacable in a men's plaid overcoat that she wore as a bathrobe, holding aloft, like a smashed Statue of Liberty, her mug, which held coffee, two shots of Jack Daniels, and three teaspoons of sugar. At forty, she could pass for thirty, but something new has settled into her face in the past few years—a watchfulness, a measure of something unspent. Allison isn't exactly sure when Tuley quietly and firmly took her place, but she did. Tuley has told Allison that she's writing a memoir. She might even write two. She wanders around the house all day, dictating her life into a handheld tape recorder.

Allison and her mother sat down in two orange bucket seats inexplicably clamped to each other near the ticket counter. "You have to learn to read important documents more carefully," said her mother. "Isn't that part of being a paralegal?" Allison found herself explaining that she does read carefully, very carefully. Her voice started to rise, and she inwardly cringed to hear herself tell a stupid tale of how, recently, were it not for her eagle eye and keen ability to spot an error, one of Buckley and Baines's clients might have been undercharged by five thousand dollars.

Regrettably, she heard herself add, "No small amount, that!"

Her mother nodded assent, but the reaction seemed weak to Allison. She could feel herself tumbling downhill inside, on the verge of coughing up other examples. Allison straightened her embroidered cap. Rounded, it rose up in the front and featured multicolored panels that gave the impression of a stained-glass window turned into a hat. Back in California it had seemed irreverent and stylish. Here in Logan Airport, it felt too bright, too large. She might as well have had an Easter basket on her head.

She doesn't offer up her history degree and teaching credential as an indication of past good reading skills, because if she did her mother would say, "What have you done with them?" But it's not that simple to Allison. She does not want to work at a museum of history or teach history or make history. She simply likes to read about it and has a burning, quiet hope of, once and for all, getting things straight.

Besides, there's comfort in saying one is a paralegal. People seem to respect it and always ask things like, do paralegals know as much as lawyers? Do paralegals have to go to a special school? And, don't paralegals have to type really, really fast?

By that point, Allison will have escaped into a thorough description of being a paralegal, forsaking any talk about the very thing she loves. She is as protective of her knowledge about the huge and infinite mash of history as if it were a single slender story, one likely to slip away at any second, or worse, be remembered incorrectly.

"American flight 409 is now boarding at gate 32," roared the overhead speaker.

Allison jumped up as if this might be her plane. No luck. She sat back down and crossed one arm over her chest, cradling her elbow in her fingertips—an indefinite sort of way to hold oneself. She often has the look of a person waiting for her coat.

"Allison, are you cold? I know we can't compete with that California vacation air," said Camille. She put her arm around Allison's back and gently tapped her fingertips.

At that moment Allison would have liked to tell Camille (but of course she didn't) that most recently she has been working as a paralegal not in a law firm, but at the Public Storage training facility in Burbank, a strange place that features a mock Public Storage service desk where trainees take turns pretending to purchase tape, boxes, and labels from each other. Primarily she explains employees' contracts to them. There is an oddly threatening and rigid quality to the atmosphere. On the kitchen wall is posted a warning that reads in foot-high letters: NO BARGING. In the women's restroom there are posters over the toilets that say, "Thank you for not flushing with your feet! It makes a difference!"

"So you see, I personally saved the firm five thousand dollars," Allison repeated.

"One should always read important documents carefully," replied her mother. Camille's hand flew to her throat, a sort of self-strangulation gesture that Allison knows her mother uses when she has plenty more to say—but would, for Allison's benefit, refrain.

"Paging Mark Riley, Mark Riley." The woman on the loudspeaker sounded delighted to say his name, as if she were calling her husband to dinner. Allison searched the waiting room to see if someone stood, though no one moved.

"Where could Tuley be?" Allison's mother said, as if Tuley didn't habitually vanish in public places. Last fall, when Allison came home, they'd gone to visit historic Old Ironsides, where Tuley promptly disappeared, somewhere onboard they thought. But long after the boat closed and the actors dressed as sailors left for the day and headed down the gangplank toward the Pirate's Stash for a beer, Allison and her mother sat there on the dock. It was in the bar, two hours later, that Tuley was recovered, spotted by Camille, who had gone in to call the police.

"Well, Tuley said she was thirsty," Camille added.

"Tuley said she needed a *drink,*" said Allison.

"Do you think she went for a Coke?"

"There are Cokes right here, if she wanted a Coke," Allison replied.

Allison knew there would be no mention of Tuley's other public disappearances, such as the time they found her passed out cold in the ironsmith's shop at Sturbridge

Village, or the incident at the Red Sox game when she appeared to hallucinate in the Fenway Park women's room and, glued to a toilet seat, thought she was driving home.

"Maybe she spotted those shoes that she's been looking for," said Allison's mother. "Or maybe something just caught her interest." Meaning a man.

A woman wearing a business suit hurried by, pulling a piece of luggage that was stamped *Useless if Delayed*.

Allison's mother began to tell the story (one she had frequently told to Allison in the last couple of years) of a time when at thirty-one (Allison's age now) she still lived with her parents in Raleigh, North Carolina. And the story was about a day when she'd been walking through a forest that bordered a churchyard. She was sad, sad because she had no husband. No mention of the fact that she'd been hospitalized for a nervous condition that involved not sleeping for weeks and the loss of chunks of her hair, a fact she hid with hats and falls.

Camille has always had this ability to till her own memory, to roll and refine it, turning a blind eye to the heavy, unending daily dirt of things, spying only the muddy coin or pretty piece of bottle glass that flies by too fast for catching. The one that serves perfectly for remembrance.

At the time her mother figured the no-husband problem was due to 1) a peculiar reserve that made her (she thought) come off as unknowable and skittish, and 2) other numerous inexplicable personality traits that she was desperate to improve, if only she could locate them. This part, as well, was never mentioned in the telling, for Allison's mother has never been able to face or let go of a crooked idea, one that has directed almost every action in her life—an aching, bottomless notion of *lesser than*.

Apparently, at the moment she got to the forest border, she saw a wedding procession on its way to the church.

"And can you imagine what I did next? I followed right along after them." Indicating that maybe, at least for a sliver of time, Camille fell in with all kinds of easy joy and did-n't brace against or approach too fast the things that came her way. "I got invited to the reception, and even danced with the groom. And I met my very own husband at that wedding. Can you believe it?"

Camille rarely mentions her husband's death or the accident that caused it. The day she met him is what she talks about.

"Anything is possible," Allison said. She looked out the window—gray. Perhaps a shade lighter than it had been this morning. And in a few hours it would be darker gray. She longed for a California sky, a sky that when she left last Thursday evening was still a trustworthy blue, streaked, as if by so many lipsticks, pale pink, peach, and raspberry.

Allison and Camille fell silent. However, they each dutifully looked up every time a blast of words rushed through the loudspeakers as if, just this once, a clear and helpful personal directive would be offered.

"Hasn't Tuley been gone over an hour?" said Allison. "Well over an hour?" she added.

But then suddenly, there she was. Tuley, in Allison's old chartreuse bell-bottoms and jean jacket, her wild red hair captured in a chip clip. Tuley stomped along in sloppy-looking sandals that belied the actual smallness of her feet, feet she often whipped out at bars, comparing their length to tall men's fingers. From ten feet off, Allison could smell Tuley's "signature fragrance," Drakkar Noir, which she sprayed inside the waistbands of her pants.

Tuley reported that she had two "worthless cocktails" in one of the airport bars. "Amateur," she declared, referring to the bartender. With her other hand hidden inside her jacket pocket, she fiddled with her good luck charm, an old motel key she called "the key to happiness." Not bothering to ask for an update on Allison's flight, Tuley started talking about how much her toes hurt and how happy she'd be once she found those sandals that she told Camille "would stay put even when bombs go off," as if she were a foreign correspondent.

After college, Tuley had "wisely used" (as Camille would say) her English degree working as a copy editor at a local newspaper. Apparently, she retired at twenty-eight. Severe allergies. Migraines. Weak knees that one time rendered her incapable of leaving a mall. Tuley has often been rushed to the hospital. Allison's mother listened carefully while Tuley explained that the last time she was in the ER a nurse stole her sandals.

"Why not just skip the ambulance rides?" asked Allison.

"I can't help that I attract emergencies," Tuley responded. The way she said the word, she could be speaking of good fortune. She blinked, and Allison noticed that Tuley had only applied makeup to one eye. And she put great care into that right side. A trio of turquoise, silver, and emerald fanned out to the tip of her eyebrow. Her left eye looked out at Allison, defenseless and unadorned, and it was easier to read her look, the one she often wore that said, "Who will ever know my side of things?"

Allison remembered the time she and her mother had visited Tuley for her nineteenth birthday at Salem State College, a school supposedly chosen for its English literature classes, but in truth, for its Salem witch cachet. Allison had been eleven.

Allison and her mother had walked into Tuley's dorm, passing no one but a woman in red corduroys who was taking fervent inventory of a supply closet, totting up marks on a clipboard and ardently pushing around bottles of Windex, whispering numbers, determined in the face of a dateless Saturday night.

They headed up the stairs, and it seemed as if a party had ended just moments ago, simply rolled up and moved on in search of higher festive ground. There was a half-eaten roll of Lorna Doone cookies on the windowsill and a L'eggs Pantyhose egg delicately placed atop an overflowing garbage can. Wet towels were carelessly dropped, left lumped in the corner of the stairwell, and a cloud of some healthy cologne, one that smelled like honey and mint, hung weakly in the face of a larger moving front of shampoo, french fries, and cigarette smells. Everyone had been rushing. Everyone was gone.

But Tuley was there. Tuley was in her room, sitting on the floor with the door open about six inches, that measure not openly hopeful of visitors, but the exact distance of practiced wishfulness—a distance that equaled exactly the length of "just in case." Tuley was untangling a beautiful silver chain with a needle, and next to her on the floor, piled in a bandana, were other chains and beads and one link bracelet, all of them devilishly snarled. Flushed, she looked up and stared at Allison and her mother in the doorway. Tuley was rigid with effort, as if deep inside herself she'd thrown her full weight against a door, one that threatened to break open any second. "Everyone gives them to me," said Tuley. "I'm good at this." It wasn't long before Tuley moved in with Allison and her mother.

"Tuley, do you think they might have those sandals you want in the new wing?" said Camille.

"But you can shop for sandals anytime," said Allison, even though there wasn't a single other thing for them to do. Two flights had arrived, another had boarded and gone. It was almost noon, and the waiting area was empty except for Tuley, Allison, and Camille, who all stood facing the main airport lobby.

"Oh, come on, let's do it," said Camille. "Let's take a chance!"

They crossed the lobby and walked beneath a grand archway. Before them lay a number of shops whose muted fronts seemed to strike the perfect balance between smugness and practicality. Tuley lifted her arms, knocking askew Allison's hat. Although the passing pilots stared at Tuley, she kept her arms raised at an angle, seemingly exultant over an airport that was designed for her enjoyment.

Allison's mother walked slightly behind Allison and Tuley, commenting in front of a purse store that displayed in its window a few pairs of shoes, "Maybe they have those sandals you want in there, Tuley." But of course Tuley had already passed it. This was part of the Tuley windup; she liked to feign disinterest in the very thing she wanted, often leading her to get more of what she desired and better than she'd originally hoped for. Or that's how it always seemed to Allison.

Tuley chatted along, repeating an old story about how when she worked at the newspaper, she'd once found a packet of cocaine wrapped in the sports page. Not that she sampled it or anything. She talked so quickly, she was almost breathless. Allison knew that Tuley took various powerful prescription medicines and/or recreational drugs.

Sometimes these made her act startled and exuberant, often followed by a period when she would brood and hatch theories about local cover-ups, spending hours at a time reading a magazine to which she had a lifetime subscription, *National Police Beat*. Long gone were her Power People vocabulary lists.

"The police told me I'd probably intercepted a big drug deal. The news was huge. Huge." Tuley flung out her arms, this time knocking Allison's hat off her head. It flew behind her, and Allison couldn't see exactly where it landed in the sea of oncoming feet. For a moment it disappeared completely.

Then there was a man who stepped out of the feet, a tall man who picked up her hat and came toward her with it. It could be a crown, the way he held it. He had a good four inches on Allison, unlike most men, and stopped directly in front of her.

Allison looked at him. His eyes were a greenish brown, a soft, dependable color that reminded Allison of the eyes of a certain type of man pictured in her childhood history books, the one who was always off to the side of an illustration, carving something useful or giving the horses a drink of water.

The man stepped forward with her hat, and when Allison, still looking in his eyes, neglected to take it, he gently placed it on her head.

"Oh," said Allison. "Thank you."

"That's a wonderful hat," he told her.

"Thank you," said Camille, as if she herself had bought it.

"It's big enough," said Tuley. She stepped toward the man, too close. She hooked a thumb in her belt loop, managing to lower her bell-bottoms yet another inch to reveal a temporary Donald Duck tattoo.

"This is my aunt," Allison said, fearing he'd assume Tuley was her friend. "And this is my mother," she added.

The man stepped back, glanced at Tuley and Camille, then returned his attention to Allison. "Are you flying today?"

"Allison loves to fly!" Camille exclaimed untruthfully, as if there were nothing else of interest to mention about her.

"I think I see those sandals I want," Tuley said, wiping one hand against her temple. She'd smudged her eye makeup, and it looked like a fresh bruise beneath her right brow.

"I am flying," Allison answered him. She intended to say something about California. She intended to clarify that she didn't live here.

"Are you part of that group that's going to—" the man started.

"I can't handle these broken-down sandals another fucking second," Tuley shouted, and she yanked off her left sandal, which was barely held together with electrical tape. She shook her foot, revealing an almost black sole.

"Where did you see the sandals you wanted, Tuley, *where?*" Camille pulled her to the side.

The man looked like he was about to say something

further to Allison, and for a moment she wildly thought he might ask her to join him, wherever he was going. "Your aunt seems like a real live wire," he finally said.

A live wire—a caught, sharp brightness, a thing that can hurt, Allison thought.

The man seemed to want to come closer to her. Then Allison saw something in him: the awkward stiffening that counts as straightening for only the very tall—the wish to lift at war with the wish to lower. This was followed by the slight bow of his head, which in turn caused the upward neck pull. And then she saw the inevitable: the delicious afterslump. He might as well have kissed her. She smiled up at him.

But then the man looked behind her, and Allison turned to see Tuley leaning against the window of a shoe store, her right palm pressed to the side of her temple, crying noiselessly. They watched Camille fumble for something in her pocketbook, most likely a hard candy. She'd often said that Tuley's erratic behavior was simply due to low blood sugar.

"Well, I better let you help her," said the man, averting his eyes from Tuley. Allison had seen the look before—the embarrassment. She should say something. Something interesting. Immediately. But all she could think of was a particular soft-eyed man from her girlhood history book, one who was remembered for carving a secret word into a tree, a warning that somehow saved a woman's life, a woman to whom he was not allowed to speak but who saw the word as she passed by in her carriage. But no, that wasn't quite it. And what historical event would this have been? It seemed like something she'd misremembered from a fairy tale. But this is the thing that Allison would have liked to tell him about, and now she had said nothing. And now Tuley was crying noisily. And now the man was leaving. And now the man was gone.

Allison turned to find her mother and Tuley still outside the store.

"What is *wrong* with you?" Allison said to Tuley. "Why do you always have to make a scene?"

Tuley looked at her. "I. Need. New. Shoes." As if this purchase would somehow unsnarl her tangled past, loosen her heart for good.

Camille took Tuley by the elbow, and they headed into a store where single shoes sat atop gold pedestals. Tuley leaned into Camille, walking as if the floor were burning her feet.

Allison looked in the direction that the man went. She couldn't even remember what he was wearing. She could only recall the look in his eyes, the steadfastness. She checked an overhead clock, more than half an hour until her flight. Allison found a water fountain and took two Dramamine, as she always did before a flight. She wasn't apart from her mother and sister for more than three minutes.

But by the time she returned to the shoe store, a high-end shop with a foreign name, she found Tuley, sitting on the carpet near the cash register. "Are you all right, Miss?" she heard the store clerk say.

"Certainly," said Tuley and she gave Allison a sidelong look that seemed to say, "I am at peace no matter where I find myself in the world."

Camille held up two different sandals, modeling one on each hand mouthing, "This one? This one?" Tuley, still seated, picked at individual tufts in the beige rug.

Then Tuley stood up and began to walk toward the door of the shoe store, and she was moving luxuriantly, it seemed. She could have been a large boat setting out to sea with flags waving and all great goodness ahead of it, but a boat with a large gash in its side, for halfway across the room Tuley seemed to sink and there was a loss of purpose. Tuley briefly made a motion with her hands inside her pockets, one that looked like "Beats me." There was really no putting this part with the next. She was walking, and then she was on the ground.

There was Tuley, lying next to a large promotional boot, completely still except for her right hand, which had a life of its own, pointing and clenching, then batting and waving away, it seemed, that big stylish shoe.

"Okay, okay, I've got it," said the salesman, and he ran to the back of the store, where he grabbed a walkie-talkie off the wall.

Tuley's "key to happiness" had fallen from her jacket and landed under a chair. Allison fished it out and put it in her own pocket.

"Tuley, can you see me? Can you?" said her mother as she crouched over Tuley. For though Tuley's eyes were open and looking upward, they seemed to be turned inward, viewing a private, ecstatic vision. She did look so happy. Perhaps she saw the entirety of Logan Airport with its roof simply lifted off like a shoe box cover, and maybe most specifically she saw the snobby store clerk, a man who couldn't be bothered to greet them two seconds ago, yelling, "Someone come! This woman needs immediate attention!"

While other people took charge—one shopper hailed a security guard, and a woman in her stockings lifted Tuley's quiet hand, checking her wrist for a pulse—Allison stood off to the side. Finally, she knelt down next to her aunt and tentatively placed her fingertips on top of Tuley's left foot, which now looked childish and unthreatening.

A paramedic pushed Camille aside. His latex gloves flipped Tuley's face side to side, as if to find her most flattering profile. He shone a little light in her eyes. Camille stood up before a gathering crowd. "This isn't a free show!" she said, not loud enough for anyone to pay attention.

Tuley would, of course, be taken to some sort of secret little infirmary. Every mall, airport, and sports center had such a station—and Tuley had been to most of them. Allison and Camille would accompany her.

Allison heard the boarding announcement for her
flight. She stood up and looked out into the corridor. She
thought she saw the tall man behind a couple wearing
evening clothes. But it wasn't him. The couple rushed by,
carrying a pineapple. It was clear they were on their way
to some exciting event. Tuley moaned and Allison turned
around. Tuley, no longer gazing upward, stared directly at
Allison, and she said something that Allison took to be
"no." Allison thought that Tuley was asking her to stay. As
if it had ever been any different.

"*No,*" she thought she heard again, vehement this time.
Allison knelt close by her aunt, their heads almost touching, and she was able to hear quite clearly what Tuley had
tried to say twice before.

"Go," Tuley said. "Go." The first one was a cold slice
of anger. But in the second Allison heard something else,
something unwound—something like a benediction.

—∞—

AS THE PLANE levels out, Allison puts her hand in her
pocket and her fingertips touch something cold and metallic. She can't place it at first, until she pulls out Tuley's "key
to happiness." Allison wonders what Camille and Tuley
might be doing now. She imagines her mother and aunt
slowly walking back through the airport. Her mother will
try to find a place to have a burger, because she'll insist that
Tuley needs red meat after her collapse. Tuley will instead

talk her into going for a drink. Allison thinks of them perched on bar stools, Tuley with her little feet tucked provocatively around the rungs, her mother with legs demurely turned to the side. As much as she wanted to be free of them, for a moment she wishes she were there.

Lottie Childs rolls her cart back down the aisle, this time offering headphones and blankets. She stop and waits for an old Indian couple who struggle to get out of their seats three rows ahead of Allison. The man at the end of their aisle stands up to let them pass, ducking his head, and Allison recognizes him as the man who had captured her hat. As the plane begins to ascend, the last bit of afternoon sun lights him in profile before sliding out the window. Someone shrieks with laughter in the seat behind Allison, and he turns to look.

For a moment he simply stares at Allison, then he opens his hands in a motion that seems to say, *where* have you been?—a gesture that speaks of irritation and relief, and a certain kind of knowing. As if Allison were always doing this when they traveled together—misreading airline tickets, standing in the wrong line, sitting in the wrong row. It's this knowing that gets her. She imagines them telling people "their story" in years to come—how they met at the airport, how he saved her hat, how she thought she'd never see him again. "Remarkable," people would say. Years would pass, and they'd begin to embellish. Just a little. Frank, for that was his name, would say that he actually changed his ticket to Chicago and followed Allison onto the flight. Sometimes they'd say they met in an airport bar and Allison had pretended she was a stewardess. It would be their own private joke, this rotation of memory. And why not? Sometimes people almost meet, but don't, sometimes things change in an instant—and history is never a slender story.

ACKNOWLEDGEMENTS

I WISH TO acknowledge the following people:

My family, for everything.

Jason White, Jamyelese Stracener, Resa Blobaum, and Jacqueline Hahn for their tremendous help, faith, and support along the way.

Dylan Landis, Judith Felsenfeld, C. Kevin Smith, Jenny Berman, and Susan Morgan for their insightful critiques and encouragement.

Kirstin Ross and Claire Sullivan for pondering the fine points.

Lee Montgomery, my editor, for her talent, humor, for championing my work from the beginning, and for making it all happen.

Meg Storey, for her sharp eye and thoughtful responses.

Elyse Cheney, my agent, for taking an interest in my work early on and for her advice and support.

The Sewanee Writer's Conference and the Squaw Valley Community of Writers.

Vince Oresman, for seeing me through the last stretc this book, for finding my glasses in the most unlikely places. and most importantly for his love, understanding, abundance of great ideas, and for making me laugh every day.